Ion Manta

Crepuscular Tales.

Five novelettes.

iUniverse, Inc.
New York   Bloomington

Crepscular Tales
Five novelettes.

iUniverse books may be ordered through booksellers or by contacting:

iUniverse
1663 Liberty Drive
Bloomington, IN 47403
www.iuniverse.com
1-800-Authors (1-800-288-4677)

ISBN: 978-1-4502-2057-6 (sc)
ISBN: 978-1-4502-2058-3 (ebook)

Printed in the United States of America

iUniverse rev. date: 5/10/2010

To everyone I love.

Ah! what is not a dream by the day
To him whose eyes are cast
On things around him, with a ray
Turned back upon the past?

Edgar Allan Poe

Contents

MARATHON.

(or Break-through.)

"Oh My Lord, thank you, and hallowed be Thy Name", murmured Brad, and went on running. Instantly he felt his hope and strength restored. He stopped, and glanced back.

The gray basalt road pierced straight into the past, receding silently as it became narrower and shrouded in a bluish haze. When he retrained his sight forward, his enlarged eyes well adapted to darkness noticed a small light, suddenly twinkling so near, so luring he wanted to touch it, as an evanescent object in a beautiful dream.

"How come I've missed it?"

But then, a tedious interval of steady, well paced jogging later, long since turned into habit, Brad became again painfully aware of his doubts. The light he saw proved deceptive, farther than he thought.

"Could it been a hallucination, a concoction of my overheated, wishful mind?"

His body filled with the venom of exhaustion. This discouraged any new initiative and obliterated his just found courage. The last trace of his will melted away. He had to stop.

"This is it", he thought.

Painfully out of breath, he panted hard. At the end of his endurance, the man abandoned himself to fate.

The rain ceased. A light warm breeze, as born on a whim, rapidly dried the narrow road running uninterrupted into the horizon. At the opposite end, where the sun disappeared, the first stars twinkled feebly, one by one in the ensuing blue darkness of the outer space.

A liquefied melancholy dripped violet blue shades of paint from the sky over the vast expanse of undefined grassy fields. Brad the runner concluded:

"I must lye down right here right now."

His legs turned soft, and the man went down, a limp wet rag smack in the middle of the hard stone pavement.

At first the wretch didn't move, but soon recovering some strength, stretched out, face turned to the sky. He shut his eyes, in a vain attempt to hide his defeat and desperation, miserably set in the desolate landscape closing in above him. A sigh left his chest. His eyes reopened. Brad sat up, perhaps sparked by the never-relenting human hope, or maybe prodded by some unexplained restlessness.

Now the light was there again, alluringly flickering in the deep darkness ahead. Inexplicably, the tinny source sent out iridescent rays, only this time clear and near.

A simple lantern hung above the entrance of a smallish building, arisen suddenly as a white chalk block between the black drapes of the night engulfing everything around.

It was this modest, insignificant twinkling light that jolted our traveler to life and provided the motivation to gather his strength, and resume running. This time fortune smiled, and the man didn't have to run for long. He stopped before the building.

There he saw several darkened windows puncturing the wall evenly on both sides of the entrance, symmetrically on both floors. The lantern above the door moved in the wind, produced a vague metallic screech, and projected dizzyingly shifting light and dark bands on the ground.

For a few seconds Brad felt mesmerized.

Even in plain daylight such wicked charms could be deceptive to human senses accustomed to the ground's well known solidity –, not unlike the shape shifting shadows the sun may cast every now and then through tree branches moving in the breeze. Then why be surprised that, bewitched by the encroaching night, our poor man felt the inexplicably overpowering urge of throwing himself, body and soul, right into the bottomless dark silence of the alternating canyons the moving light so alluringly opened up for his temptation?

Had this happened our story must have ended right here. Fortunately the poor soul woke in time to the ominous nature of the strange phenomena, came quickly and shuddering to his wits, one lucky individual barely saved from the clutches of the evil lure. But, as always, there was a tradeoff.

Back in the hard reality, it didn't take the man long to feel the chill of night penetrating slowly into the sinew of his weary bones. Only a heartbeat later, he succumbed to the irrepressible need of finding a warm place for resting his body and soul. Any place. For our hungry and shivering wanderer the thought of risking another night under the vast unfriendly sky appeared suddenly unbearable.

At this very instant, Brad noticed a sign above the lantern, so timeworn that deciphering it had to be difficult even in full daylight. However, hope emboldened him now or, as some cynics might suggest, the lack of options, and the man concluded:

"This must be an inn. What else could it be?"

He grabbed the large tarnished bronze knocker, and forcefully hit twice the solid oak door, under which a thin band of yellowish light leaked out into the darkness.

"Come on in", arose from inside a sleepy nasal voice, "the door isn't locked."

Brad pushed firmly down on the handle, and cracked the door rather cautiously, hoping to soften the ensuing loud screech, of which he became almost instantly aware. Carefully alternating hesitation with action, eventually he stepped in and shut the damned door, although never to affect its murderous shriek.

"What a hellish contraption! I wonder when had it been oiled the last time?" muttered he vexed, and turned around to venture further in.

He found himself in a narrow, low room overheated to a feverishly oppressive temperature. Right hand side to the entrance, a single dusty, fly-speckled light bulb, hung above a dark-colored, weatherworn wooden counter perpendicular to the wall, vaguely illuminated this veritable lair.

Strangely foul odors and a sticky sort of moisture invaded Brad's nostrils and lungs, reminding of dirty, sweat-soaked towels left behind to stink freely in a Turkish bath. The stench at first repulsed him, but with no sensible alternative at hand, he went on.

"In my present predicament I have no choice."

He was prepared to put up with anything, only to have a roof over his head.

The man launched timidly into studying the place.

Behind the counter, Brad could sense a dark alcove as a hollow in a rotten tree, in the left corner across the room stairs, leading to the second floor. In the middle of the semi dark space between the counter and the staircase were two folding chairs and a narrow wooden table, all grimy looking under thick layers of dust. At the other side of the entrance a simple, fairly long bench, wooden too, was set against the wall possibly for the benefit of waiting customers.

"All this arrangement must have surely seen better days", the man thought, before noticing near the table a broom sticking out of a rusty bucket, obviously not used during the day, possibly not ever. Right away this lonely verticality impressed the intruder as an ominous warning of sorts.

"What a miserable abode," Brad mused involuntarily walking around in the room on time-battered clay-covered floor planks lying under the ever present dust, accumulated thicker in the corners of the whitewashed walls.

Behind the counter hang the framed portrait of a stern looking man of priestly air; to judge by the long black robe he wore. The painting seemed to be the only ornamentation in the depressingly miserable room.

Then the same funky nasal voice interrupted Brad's search, and invited him to approach the counter.

"Hey man, come over here, and stop staring at the walls as a dummy. Better tell me who you are, and what are you looking for at this late hour of night."

Brad startled first, then obeyed timidly, slightly amused at hearing the host's unbelievably nasal voice.

"How come I didn't notice this guy behind the counter?"

"Don't bother about that, my friend. Don't rack your brain with stupid questions. I was just reclining on my bed. You couldn't see me", intervened the almost invisible host proving able to read his guest's mind. "Come nearer, I want to look you in the eyes."

Marveling a little on the man's ability to read thoughts Brad approached slowly. Once there, behind the counter he saw the bed and the lumpy hay mattress, on it a surly man, casting a large vague shadow on the wall.

Obviously he just sat up. His long whitish hair and beard looked disheveled; the eyes were visible only as dark holes. Clad in a gray coarse cassock of burlap tied around the waist by a soiled piece of old rope, the man kept his hands neatly clutched on his lap, near a bunch of large, dangling keys.

"Good evening", Brad spoke in a low voice, then somewhat firmer: "My name is Brad, Brad Constant, and I would like to spend the night in this inn. Can I have a bed? I am week, cold, exhausted, and hungry. I'd be grateful for getting a warm soup too."

He turned silent; his own courage all of a sudden scared him, as it often happens to the timid dropped in unexpected trouble.

"Hmm, yes, yes - in this inn -," grumbled the man muffled, and moved to the bed's edge, shaking his head as one utterly familiarized with the approach of the helpless guy before him. But then he concluded on a friendlier tone: "Well, well my friend, couldn't you find a more decent time than to wake me up at midnight?"

Without waiting for the reply the host began cracking meticulously his backbone, evidently trying to chase sleep off his unawake body, bothered in the least by the presence of his late visitor.

Faced with this, ignored and guilt ridden, Brad launched into some impossibly formal excuses:

"Mr. Superintendent, please forgive me; I tried hard to arrive earlier, at a more decent time, but since I lost my way in the fields—"

His effort proved futile. The host's vaguely rhetoric question didn't require a logical reply. But our intruder, as most involuntary trespassers, strove by all means to be exceedingly polite.

"Okay, okay, I know: all late comers will find some valid excuse, won't they?" Then, a short pause later he went on, adopting an obviously sarcastic ton:"I must confess, though, that I find it extremely difficult for anyone to miss his way on the only road leading to us."

Brad, aggressed as he felt under the torrent of undeserved sarcasm, dropped his gaze. He attempted vainly to hide his hurt, still intent on explaining himself.

"What you said surely rings true; however, I don't really know whether I intended to arrive here at all."

Convinced that frankness could work in his favor, by the time his last words left his lips he regained a modicum of self-assurance and calm. But then, only an instant later, his heart sank nearly stopped in fear, when the innkeeper turned with renewed anger against him in his familiarly exaggerated nasal and harsh tone of voice.

"Mr., a-a-a--…. what did you said your name is?

"Br--, Br--, Br--, Brad, Brad Constant," he finally stammered off his name.

"Well, well, listen Mr. Brad Constant, and listen well. Do not even try imagining I appreciated you smart-Alec remark. Our place is not at all a shelter, thus it has no room whatsoever for wandering vagabonds needing temporary refuge for the night." Then he fired off the next question, harshly, machinegun-like, without any further ado; "Where do you come from?"

"From Demlica, Rombardia."

"Can you prove it?"

"Yes, sir," but when Brad was about to take out his papers, the host stopped him.

"No need for that now. Where are you headed?"

"I haven't decided yet. I am disoriented a bit, you see my information is fragmented and _" - a short pause later —"in fact, that's why I came. May I ask where should I really go?"

"Huh yes, isn't he smart? Look at him, how well he learned his lines," muttered softly the host, and stretched out on the mattress, suddenly feigning boredom.

No longer paying attention to his visitor, he returned to cracking bones, especially his long fingers, one by one, probably engaged in a mental search for further questions, preparing to dart off new ones, without sitting up. This happened, too, a little later.

"Let me then skip the details, and ask you directly. Do you wish to go in Newland, don't you?

However, now it was his turn to be surprised, after hearing Brad spit off a new question in lieu of a response.

"What's life like in that part of the world? Is it good?"

"Ouch, this guy is less stupid than he looks, and every now and then can be quite fresh," the host mused, fixed his gaze apparently interested on his guest, and answered.

"Frankly, I don't know. On the other hand, I can assure you that almost everyone landing here heads exactly to that land, to Newland."

Brad absorbed the bit of information in silence that lasted quite a time. During the ensuing eerily tranquil interval he involuntarily returned to scanning objects in the room, which suddenly appeared even sadder, miserably yellowier and dirtier than before. Eventually he exploded, almost insolently:

"And what happens if I won't like it in Newland? Is there a way back to this place?"

Suddenly, the official acting as the reception officer, burst into a hearty laughter. His visitor's sneaky question obviously sounded amusing to his experienced ears.

"The poor guy wants to find out what awaits him in the future. Ha!" But while entertaining this thought, he probably searched for some noncommittal answer.

"Strange question! Naturally, anyone can change his mind, and turn back from almost anyplace, don't you think? But, I must forewarn you that returning is seldom advisable; it almost never ends up well for the undecided."

A long pause ensued during which Brad appeared rooted to the ground, totally dumbfounded. He didn't fancy at all the desk officer's answer. He hoped for something altogether different, definitely for more encouraging words. Instead, the official gave him nothing, no useful advice other than philosophical generalities, commonplaces, things he was well aware of too. But, sensing the weight of silence in the room grow overly heavy, he eventually forced himself to utter somewhat haltingly a rhetorically insipid question, as someone unable to produce a wittier answer to an obvious banality:

"And so, what's a man in my position to do?"

Taking stock of the question, the desk officer sat up on his bed, and after a short search under the counter, came up with some printed forms, an indelible marker pen, then fixed his eyes straight into Brad's:

"In other words," he placed a meticulous stress on the syllables, "you did decide to go in Newland, right?

Brad's previous semblance of certainty suddenly evaporated. He wasn't prepared to agree to anything precise about a choice as yet unknown to him. Attempting subconsciously to diffuse somehow the new awkward situation, he proceeded, for better or worse, to rub nervously his hands, as if not knowing what to do. But he kept obstinately silent.

"Mister Brad, you may go wherever you please," cut in the desk officer again, apparently realizing his guest's dilemma.

He reverted to his nasal voice, and became extremely polite, perhaps a tad pedagogical.

"We in this country can't guess, nor impose solutions on anyone. Each person must choose his own peculiar destination, you know." At this point the host sighed, shrugged his shoulders, and went on with a nuance of insinuation, "In the last resort, you could stay here, in our village, in which case__ "

At this bit of new information, Brad jumped in with another question, greedy and impatient, the very man trying to catch the last hope of an unexpected but acceptable escape out of a dilemma.

"Well, what would happen to me in that case? May I know?"

"Oh, that depends."

"Depends on what?"

Brad's obviously overt curiosity prompted the official to a renewed offensive in vagueness and ambiguity, emphasized by an increasingly slower speaking rhythm.

"It depends, first of all - I said it before -, on your own choice, and on some intricate details. Tell me right now straight, can you finally decide on whatever it is you exactly want?"

Running hopelessly on empty again, caught in a vicious circle, Brad no longer saw any way out of his predicament. Thoroughly confused, absolutely incapable of arriving at a rational decision, reduced to the level of an object exposed to the whims of a game, but fighting to free his mind from these constraints, he almost yelled his well-syncopated answer.

"I am going to Newland!"

"Hmm. How typical," acknowledged the man in cassock, and regained his dour but indifferent attitude, of the official exercising his duty. "You behave exactly, but exactly as all the others. First you ask to the left of target, then you ask to the right of it, abuse the precious time of a public official - because, you know, that's who I am - only to end up smack where I assumed you'd go from the beginning. Phew, disgusting!"

The man's face stretched into long grimace of obvious disdain and undisguised disappointment. A short halt later, purposefully inserted for dramatic effect, he asked:

"Tell me then man, why did you play the fool, why did you have to be so shamelessly perfidious in dealing with me?"

The official affixed anew his gaze right between the eyes of his late visitor, and smiled ironically, without the slightest intent of disguising his contempt.

And Brad, back in a bind, had no choice but to resist, this time trying not to blink, of course in vain. Luckily for him, the official did not prolong the scene needlessly. He placed the papers on the counter, almost disappeared under it, only to reemerge with a new set of printed forms unceremoniously handed to his late-night visitor.

"Here, read the questions carefully, and fill in your answers as precisely and honestly as you can. Withholding the truth for a person in your condition can prove quite costly. Believe me, I am not joking. Make sure you won't omit any question."

At this the man halted, as if to increase the importance of what he just said, then added, while pointing straight out with his index finger.

"And now have a seat at the table you see over there, and set to work diligently. Use only the ink and pen provided for this purpose. Any questions?"

Brad did not find any, but kept staring benumbed at the man behind the counter. By now he involuntarily took the military stance of attention, afraid even to blink.

Seeing this new attitude the clerk concluded his mission, apparently and momentarily satisfied by his performance and achievement, but not before saying:

"When you're finished, approach my desk, and I will tell you what to do next. Okay?"

Without any further ado he reverted to his usually bland and indifferent bearing, stretched out on the bed, and pulled the coarse blanket over his head. A minute later, the healthy and honest gurgling music of his snoring flooded the room.

Brad, still helplessly rooted on the spot before the counter finally lowered his gaze on the forms in his hands. He shuffled the paper sheets several times, and then tried to read some of the questions in a haphazard manner.

At first he could barely comprehend any. The questions seemed unnecessarily lengthy and much too complicated.

"This looks as a hellish job to do," thought he suddenly saddened, "especially on an empty stomach and with a sleepy head." A deep sigh escaped his chest. "At least the room is warm and relatively comfortable, certainly more so than the outdoors."

He remembered that only half an hour earlier he'd given the world for a warm putrid hole in a tree trunk, just to avoid the night's desolation and the chilly North-Easterly wind blowing over the open fields.

Slowly he headed for the indicated spot. He walked softly, tepee toeing, extremely careful not to wake the slumbering clerk, now in retrospect, appearing to him quite benevolent. In the same cursed instant he realized how badly the dry clay-covered floor planks screeched under his steps, making an infernal noise he didn't pick up before.

This new failure made our character painfully aware of his wretched existence. The screeching grew unbearable, amplified to a terribly cosmic magnitude, associated inexplicably to some uniquely isolated and violent events in the Universe, closing in from above, scratching the surface of Brad's brain as a dulled record player's needle glide on a worn record.

Be that as it may, he reached the table without other incidents. Fortunately, the clerk's uninterrupted snoring covered most noises.

This allowed Brad to sit down successfully on the folding metallic chair at the table. Victorious at last, he exhaled a deep sigh of relief. Then, after finding a minimum of comfort, he set himself to the task of familiarizing with the writing tools at hand.

First, he opened the inkwell; second, he picked up the primitive looking pen; third, he dipped it carefully in the watery blue ink, intent on drawing a few straight lines on the white paper sheet on top of the pile, just to test how the writing tool worked.

To his bitter annoyance, just as he was about to draw the second line, a fat drop of ink insidiously dripped from the crooked pen's tip, to spread rapidly in all directions as the nastiest infectious disease, and create a bedbug-like big ugly blotch on the immaculate whiteness of the sheet.

"Gosh", he hissed in frustration, wishing never to been born.

But all was for naught. The accident occurred, and - anyone knows - the past is irretrievable.

"It serves me right. The clerk informed me all right about the ill-fated consequences of my actions, when undertaken thoughtlessly. Too bad I didn't heed his advice. Now I must get serious, and proceed with super-extra caution."

Satisfied with his new attitude, the man resolved to no longer postpone his task, and set right then to work on the damned forms. He barely finished the thought, and a renewed numbness invaded his tired body.

"Maybe I should take a little nap first, to clear my mind. Then again, I might not wake up, and the morning could catch me sleeping, with my work not yet done? How will the clerk judge me then? No way. I can't risk it. I must finish the job now. Period."

This miraculously regained resolve perked him up, and he commenced reading.

"Last name. First name. Date and place of birth." BRAD, COSTANT, 15th of MAY 19--.

He shaped nice capital letters quickly, in conformity to the instructions, and as he finished the first line, said:

"Hmm, why did this appear so difficult just a minute ago? The task is actually simple. I can finish my work in a jiffy, and still have plenty of time left for a nap."

On pondering such reassuring thoughts, Brad felt again that unmistakably terminal lightness insinuate into his limbs, and his mind almost blacked out, as hit by a strong shot of sweet brandy, when sipped after a copious meal. The sensation quickly turned off his just found assurance.

When he tried to read on, the letters suddenly changed colors, from black-to-green-to blue, only to violently shake before his achy eyes. The words danced in sad, macabre, syncopated rhythms. Feeling the entire world slip irresistibly away, the man struggled and gave all he's got in a last desperate attempt. Thus he succeeded in filling a few more lines.

"Nicknames used, height, weight, color of eyes, other distinguishing marks, and so on."

Struggling thusly he answered all questions on the first page. He went on to the next.

"List all residences of the last five years, then years of schooling - grammar school, middle school, college, university, postgraduate studies."

Next came the chapter about his ancestry: "Name of parents - father's name, mother's maiden name, name of maternal and paternal grandparents" - and so on, in this exact order.

At this point Brad raised one eyebrow and caught himself quietly cursing all the nonsense, all the useless byproducts of bureaucracy, in his opinion, so well perfected everywhere in the world, regardless of the country's size or importance.

"I wonder what the hell they want with my grandmother's name."

He inhaled deeply, and went on.

"Job history in order, beginning with the last or, if applicable, with the present one."

Although fairly simple, the questions demanded concentration. At the next line the whole affair turned outright impossible, demanding attention to detail, and a perfect memory. Such data, hard to remember under normal condition, becomes even more so in the midst of a sleepless night.

The pen fell from Brad's hand causing a minuscule tap when it hit the table.

"I wonder, what happens to all the little noises never recorded, but randomly dispersed in the Universe?"

By the time he finished munching on this somewhat absurd but philosophically familiar thought, the man's head grew so heavy that he felt the irrepressible need to let it rest - a lead ball squeezed between his elbows set firmly on the table. Brad slowly passed into that unfathomable void of oblivion, whereby no one demands good answers to senseless questions. Overtaken by exhaustion he fell asleep - deeply, thoroughly, almost lethally knocked out.

He didn't sleep for long. At least that's what he thought when the hellishly furious and loud clang of an alarm clock shaking on a shelf beneath the priestly looking portrait woke him up brutally.

Jolted off his dream, the man sprung up behind the table as pulled by a string. Helpless, the insane marionette forced lately to become in the cruel game of life, he began gesticulating in silence, trying in vain to stop the noise – so-to-speak - telekinetically, and prevent waking the cassocked clerk, sleeping behind the counter. Every now and then a man's action can be so futile!

The alarm clock did its job well; its ear-piercing racket woke the clerk.

The official jumped reflexively off his bed, executed an impossible somersault for a man his size, age and position, and succeeded to kill the clanging with a single skillfully administered blow with his fist on the clock's barely visible small red button. Only then, after so adroitly reestablishing the welcome peace and quiet in the room, he turned his attention to his guest, and addressed him quite reproachfully.

"Obviously it is not enough for you to wake me, but you won't be happy before disturbing everyone else in the building. Am I right?"

"Please mister manager, I implore you from the bottom of my heart to forgive me. I didn't do it on purpose; really, I can't imagine why I have not seen the alarm clock in the first place. Please, please, forgive me."

Evidently the man verged on loosing his mind. Terrified and confused he babbled on.

"I know; I know I am guilty. I should have noticed the alarm clock up there, since I have eyes, as you can see yourself. I am honestly sorry, please forgive me. I beseech you."

"Yeah, yeah, yeah, apology accepted, although you should have noticed the clock all right." Adopting a softer attitude, he added almost as an afterthought. "Unfortunately no one likes to take note of time, or its measurer, large as it obviously looms on life. Look at it, man! At last now, can't you see the clock on the shelf?"

"Oh yes, yes, I see it quite clearly. How beautifully luminous its white face shines in the dark. My lack of attention is inexcusable. I don't know what else to say."

"Okay, okay, you're forgiven. But now do me the favor, and stop your idiotic lamentations. The alarm clock, anyone can see, has been on the wall all the time, ticking on duty in the same spot. Remember that always! Okay?"

Although the clerk's anger subsided rapidly, he grew bitter and disappointed. Brad noticed the change, the small amount of cold acquiescence in the man's voice, and his courage returned almost instantly.

"I will remember your advice for ever. I promise."

A long silence descended in the room, during which the clerk kept gazing at his guest almost expressionless. Ill at ease under the overt pressure of this voided gaze, Brad decided timidly to change the subject.

"Sir, may I ask something?"

"Okay, okay, you may, but please be succinct. It is getting late, and I am sorely tired."

"Could you tell me sir, who is the guy in the picture above the clock? He emphasized his question pointing at the portrait.

"That guy, huh? You said the guy, ha, ha, ha, that guy, isn't it?

The cassocked clerk repeated the words several times, gradually with increased oomph, barely able to withhold his laughter. Then pointing and gazing alternately to the picture and to Brad, he finally let go.

"Ha, ha, ha, the guy, as you call him my friend, is the Big Boss. You know, it could well happen one of these days for you to need him badly. In your place I'd be rather more respectful when referring to him as *that guy.*"

Slapped again into submission, Brad lowered his head in frustration. He seriously began to doubt his wits, painfully aware of the precariousness of his stance. The new gaffe he committed on the account of a senseless curiosity sparked him that instant to refrain from ever speaking before seriously premeditating on the issue at hand.

The clerk, seeing his victim so thoroughly shook up and defeated, continued unmoved the pressure of his scrutiny a little longer, then apparently satisfied by his tactics, perhaps tired by the game, retreated slowly behind the counter, stretched out lazily on the mattress, and asked, as if nothing happened.

"Did you finish filling the forms I gave you?"

And to his chagrin, our victim had once again to find out that regardless of how hard he tried being correct, he always ended up in trouble. Thus he could do nothing but revert to his usual excuses.

"I was about to finish my task, when I don't know why and how, maybe because I've been so exhausted, I fell asleep. I beg for your forgiveness. Please give me another chance, ten minutes or so, to complete the job. I have less than two pages to fill. Sir, do I have your permission to resume work? I am prepared to start right now."

"Ah, the hell with it. Hand me the papers as they are, filled or unfilled. Look, soon it is dawn; we must have some rest. Don't you agree?"

"Yes Sir, I do. But let me see if I understand it correctly; you want me to turn in the forms, even if incomplete?"

"Exactly."

Surprisingly, the clerk no longer spoke nasally, but quite casually, on a normal, decent and benevolent tone of voice.

"It is more important for the papers to be registered than to be fully completed. You know my friend, there'll be always time for additions later."

Perplexed, absolutely snarled in the new twist, Brad hastily gathered the partially filled forms, stacked them neatly in a pile, which he picked up, and quickly delivered to the clerk, who sat up on the edge of his bed, his hand stretched out in acceptance.

Caught between curiosity, prudence and fear, all experienced at the same time, Brad timidly asked, after handing over his papers.

"Sir, could you tell me, what would be the repercussions of having a file with documents only partially complete?"

"No repercussions whatsoever my friend. Don't worry about such trifles. Let me tell you in confidence that it could be quite beneficial for a man in tight position to have a little wiggle room for maneuvering. I'm sure you understand this much, don't you?"

The clerk winked once or twice, and his tone betrayed a clear nuance of benevolent complicity.

"Yes, yes, sir, I think I understand," admitted Brad somewhat reluctantly although no longer comprehended anything at all, but resolved to stand his ground by staring straight into the luring dark void behind the clerk. From the corner of his eyes he could see the official fish beneath the counter, and bring to light a badly soiled calendar and a stubby indelible marker, to register the documents with a tedious and pedantic expertise under the proper date and place. Then he grabbed an unusually big rubber stamp, moistened it with his breath twice, and applied it forcefully and noisily on the lower left corner of the top sheet, to finish the job.

"Yes, that's it. We did good work. My friend now I must go upstairs, and wake up the superintendent, in case you didn't do it already with the alarm clock." But before proceeding, he turned to Brad. "As for you, I would strongly advise to make yourself scarce, at least for a while. Find some useful thing to do, for instance, pick up a little sleep, or whatnot. By the way, are you hungry? Oh, what am I asking? Of course you are. You must be famished as a wolf. How much money you have?"

"I don't have any money at all."

"Of course you don't have money. Who in your predicament has? But I suppose you did held on to your number, didn't you?"

"What number?"

"Look man; don't play the fool with me. Must you always get on my nerves? What number, what number? You need a number, the admittance number. Comprende? You had taken one before entering the office, haven't you? They were readily available at the door."

"No, I didn't. I've seen no such things out there. I don't have a number."

"O-My-God, this is precisely how everyone of your ilk plays on my patience. Man, man, what do you expect to eat if you don't have a number? What do you think; you just go to the mess hall and eat, just like that?

"Sir, please forgive me again, I am a novice. Can I get out, and pick a ticket now?"

"What, are you crazy? Nobody can go out, and come in again. Don't you know?"

"Then how may I get the number? Or, if I can't, what now?"

"Well, rest assured we would take care of that at the proper time, naturally, when your situation will have cleared. The question is what should I do with you now? You must eat, don't you?"

This time the priestly clerk appeared honestly dumbfounded, as he kept bobbing slowly his head. Following some deep pondering, finally he came up with the saving grace. First he turned to Brad:

"When did you eat for the last time?"

"Two days ago."

"God! The same story, as a broken record played over and over again. Hey people, why the hell don't you learn to leave home with some victuals in your bags? Can't you figure how long the trip might be? It is harder and harder for me to feed all you vagrants off my modest salary. One day I have to make it clear; I must follow the rules as everyone else here. I could end up in real trouble for helping the likes of you. Besides, my wife could be fed up too, and eventually push me on the street, if I kept bringing her too many uninvited customers such as you."

The man looked sincerely distressed, as he kept bobbing his head mechanically some more.

"Well, the hell with the rules!" he exploded eventually resigned to his fate, and spit out a little quieter a hardly reproducible curse between his teeth. Then abruptly changing course he continued.

"Refugee Brad, go to my wife. She works in the kitchen by the officer's mess hall. She will surely find some scraps for you, maybe a piece of bread and some leftover cheese, probably enough to tie you over for a while. Tell her I've sent you. In the meantime I will present your case in the best possible light to my superior officer. We share lunch and a glass or two of wine together." Here the clerk stopped as if trying to remember something, then added: "Go, and don't be afraid. Things have a strange way of always getting resolved somehow."

The clerk winked in the same complicit fashion as before, took Brad's file under his armpit, turned on his heels, and arriving at the foot of the staircase, stopped to turn his head at his customer, rooted to the spot in disbelief.

"Ah, there is something else. When you finished eating, please be good, and get out in the yard, and start running circles around the building. Make sure you run, not just walk in a leisurely pace. Don't stop for anything, not even for a blink, regardless of how tired you'll feel. Do you un-der-stand?"

"Yes sir, I do," yelled Brad involuntarily as a soldier would before an officer, but right then, when noticed the momentary expression of stupefaction on the clerk's face, added in a softer, more restrained voice. "Hey good fellow, thank you."

"Now listen man, and listen well. To you I am not a *fellow*, neither good, nor bad. So from now on, I would appreciate if you address me properly as '*Mr. Concierge*'. No more, no less. Okay? And now go, what are you waiting for?"

Brad lowered his gaze to his worn-out shoes, and felt deeply ashamed. He almost blew it again, because of his misplaced expression of gratitude, which could have been easily interpreted as insolence, or abuse of his benefactor's goodwill.

When he raised his eyes the clerk was gone. Having nothing more to do, he slowly recapitulated the clerk's instructions, and then set off to find the mess hall.

Soon he came upon it too, and as promised, the concierge's wife served him without uttering a word some morsels of bread and cheese. With his belly properly mollified, he remembered the clerk's advice, and went out into the open.

An enormous sun sent its first rays over the vast waist-land, gilding everything with a dusting of pink gold as far as the eye could see.

New hope filled Brad's chest. He drew a deep breath of fresh air, and begun his first tour running around the building, as ordered.

*

Now, in the glaring morning's sunlight, Brad could see a tinny village having a few dozens whitewashed houses with straw thatched roofs, all surrounded by well-kept, similarly sized and shaped kitchen gardens.

"So this is my salvation," he quipped inexplicably cheered, although he didn't truly know much of anything about it as yet; how this new world worked, what it could offer. Ah, the inextinguishable human hope!

The dusty grayish road he traveled last night ended abruptly in the so-called inn that is in the administration building, the sole imposing structure in the small hamlet. In the opposite direction, the road receded silently back to the East, gradually narrowing by twists and turns until it vanished at the hazy horizon, where the rusty fields met the blue ink of the sparkling sky.

"Who could say what lay beyond that line? Perhaps not even I", mused Brad wondering before falling back definitely into the present.

The village lay island-like amidst a sea of grass, punctured here and there by few shrubs, and one large, lonely, almost leafless tree, showing to the sun its blindingly white, wind-polished bark.

Brad took note of this superb but crushing landscape while running, willfully repressing his bone and muscle's insistent protests brought about by the sleepless night. He paused to take off his shoes, and cool his feet a bit. Then he quickly resumed running barefoot through the wet grass - shoes tied around his neck by the laces.

The cool fresh air, the bright light, the soothing effect of dewdrops flowed up through the shin, tie bone, and the spine straight into his heart, contrasting sweetly with the warmth of bread and cheese working wonders in the stomach. The feeling gave him wings. Thusly he ran; new hope and unbelievable will to live invigorated his whole being.

"This is not too bad" he mused. "Only if I had slept a little everything could be better than fantastic."

Suddenly he recalled his mishap with the alarm clock. The night's adventure made him burst into a howl of hearty laughter. He laughed as an idiot and kept running.

Fortunately no one saw him, not even the children - boys and girls with satchels carried on their backs -, joyfully streaming off their homes on the streets, probably headed for the school located somewhere in the village center.

The children passed by Brad without noticing him, as if he was invisible. Somewhat intrigued, he had an idea, to stop running, and ask a boy for the village's name. Said and done. He raised one hand, signaling his innocent willingness to address the first urchin coming his way. If he only knew the huge surprise in store for him!

The instant the little boy caught sight of the stranger, his face contorted in terror, as if the poor soul saw some sort of monster. Next the same little devil swiftly turned on his heel and begun running backward, crying out as loud as he could:

"Mommy, mommy, help, help!"

At first, the boy's strange, inexplicable and unreasonable behavior didn't discourage Brad. He repeated his gesture with another kid, and met with the same result. When noticed, the children ran away, shrieking and yelling wildly terrified, as by Beelzebub himself.

"What the hell could be wrong with these bumpkins? What about my person could be so repelling to scare them so badly?" he wandered, then suddenly remembered the clerk's advice, and resumed running.

The effect ensued instantly. Just seconds earlier out of their minds with fear, the same children miraculously calmed down, and continued on their way undisturbed towards the village center.

The few mothers who came out in the street - all sporting brightly colored curlers in their hair - glanced peremptorily left, then right, and after some short, strident quips, returned to their homes, mumbling and shrugging, obviously a bit irritated by the false alarm. The heart-shrinking echoes the slamming gates caused reverberated painfully in Brad's eardrums for a while.

Peace and quiet returned to the village. No one noticed Brad's presence any longer. But he decided to act more circumspectly, and keep running without stopping - even for slowing his breath -, determined to avoid other nasty surprises. Now the man reached the point of deadlock. He was no longer aware of his exhaustion.

Reckoning by the sun's position in the sky, he guessed to have spent about two, three hours running since leaving the mess hall.

Round about this time, pondering on his apparently inexhaustible endurance, all of a sudden he got lethally thirsty. A never before experienced inner drought drained off his vitality, shriveled him dry body and soul. His mouth parched as the Sahara dunes on the sunniest days; a searing hot furnace blast scorched his throat to a rasp. As any long distance runner, he reached the stage when water became his most acute necessity, a question of life and death. Finding a source of the vital liquid had to be imminent, or else he'd die.

And then Brad the runner knew; only the purity of natural water can extinguish the fire in his guts, only this basic substance may extinguish the flames blazing in his heart, and bring tranquility to his entire being tortured by doubts. No other kind of intoxicating drink will do.

But there was more. Before he knew it, the fire in the chest turned unbearably painful, and shot razor-sharp arrows straight through the throat's gate narrowing in response to bar escape for the heart precisely when the runner's belabored breathing grew dangerously short stroked, hissing spasmodically as before expiring.

Shaken to the core, Brad intuitively cut his way across an empty lot between the houses, then through a kitchen garden, and several patches of weedy overgrowth, finally got out in the open fields surrounding the village.

By now he'd die rather than continue his run. He had to stop. At all cost.

And he did near a rickety doghouse, and a rusty pot of water, left for the apparently missing animal, but as he saw it, fate placed miraculously there for his salvation.

Although this rather unholy water meant exactly that, he still approached it with great care, while his mind worked feverishly on the hellish alternatives.

"Yes I am thirsty, this is true, but why end up bit by a dog? This would be quite unwelcome, especially in my precarious situation."

Luckily the augurs this time smiled on the runner. The doghouse looked uninhabited, the pot filled to the brim.

"This water must have accumulated during yesterday's rain," Brad reflected relieved, as the man eager to welcome a bit of solace when in dire straights.

Cautiously, he scanned the scene furtively around to make sure he was alone. Only after these precautions taken he lowered on all fours in a truly beastly fashion, and began slurping, greedy and noisy, the glassy, sun-warmed brackish water.

"Oh Lord, how sweet Thy water is!"

When halfway through the vital liquid in the pot, he heard an ominous growl, coming clearly from the doghouse. Worried anew, he lifted his head off the pot, and for a few heart-pounding seconds waited fearfully for the presumed peril.

But nothing happened. In the deep silence ruling over at grass-level he could hear the bugs swarming. Nothing else moved.

"It had to be just my imagination working overtime."

Regaining a modicum of tranquility, he sunk his head back in the pot, and did not stop slurping before he licked out the last drop.

Once his thirst had been finally extinguished, he stood up, stretched his bones and, obviously reinvigorated, resumed running.

The world seemed beautiful again, cheerful and colored with optimism. On the azure-blue sky the sun shone brilliantly, a promise-filled future slowly took shape on the screen of his mind. And soon enough, he heard a voice calling in the distance, his first name twice, only then his last once.

"Bra-a-a-d, Bra-a-a-d Constant. Where are you?"

The concierge kept yelling his name incessantly through the administration building's open doorway. The words rolled echoing over the fields in waves that multiplied the man's phony nasal voice, so annoying but by then familiar to Brad.

He quickened his pace, and soon could see the official, clad in his black cassock down to his ankles.

"Hurry up my friend, and for God's sake be a little more responsive," came his warm encouragement when Brad stopped before him. The clerk unceremoniously shouldered the poor man in, while whispering hastily in his ears, in a low but normal voice, almost in a conspiratorial manner.

"Man, how lucky can you be? You must have been born on a Sunday! The superintendent seems to be in excellent mood this morning. He wants to see you right this minute. But be careful, and refrain from the stupid answers you tried to sell me last night. This guy, unlike me, lacks any sense of humor. Remember, you must reckon with the important question of your acceptance, an issue I don't recommend gambling with. Do you understand?"

Instead of confirming verbally, Brad just nodded curtly, a little overwhelmed by the official's obvious urgency. Questions came to the tip of his tongue, he wanted some details, but he was cut short unceremoniously, and shoved impatiently up the stairs leading to the second floor. A last friendly pat firmly applied on Brad's shoulder, and the concierge concluded loudly in his official nasal tone of voice.

"Hurry up! Go to the first floor, room number three A, on the right hand side."

Brad begun climbing the stairs with hesitation, aware of the tight knot formed in the pit of his stomach. He almost heard his heart racing in his throat as he went up.

"This is it. The hour of my fate is about to strike," he thought.

Two flights later Brad came into a narrow hallway, poorly illuminated from above through a dirty window cut in the ceiling. He noticed immediately two closed, adjacent doors, and two wooden benches set against the opposite wall. Some indistinct brownish color barely transpired through both doors' and the benches' grime. Small shiny yellow rectangular bronze plaques indicated the rooms: numbers 3A, and 3B.

At last our man gathered the requisite courage to knock timidly twice on the door number 3A, as instructed. No reply came, not the slightest noise, or the tiniest movement. After some carefully calculated delay, Brad knocked again, this time more forcefully. He met with the same result. Nothing.

Unsure of the next move he just stood there, frozen motionless, pondering what to do. Finally he made up his mind, knocked for the third time, turned the knob, and prudently pushed the door in the width of a crack, prepared to cast a furtive glance inside, without any invitation.

At first the sharp light streaming out through the opening blinded him, and he could distinguish nothing. Left with no choice, he opened the door wider, and stepped in the room. The midday's brilliant sunlight flooded the office through two large, wide-open windows.

Between the windows, Brad noticed a man napping behind a large desk, his head supported on his palms. He was robed in the same black cassock as the concierge. On the highly polished but dusty desk top shone a bronze plaque, similar to those on the doors; two words clearly and deeply engraved in the yellow metal with large capital letters:

"THE SUPERINTENDENT."

Not much else in the room, aside the portrait of the same priestly figure, seen downstairs above the alarm clock. On the left hand wall Brad noticed another door - soiled and timeworn as most in the building -, he correctly assumed to lead to the adjacent room 3B. On this door the same type bronze plaque stated a warning:

"ENTRANCE PROHIBITED."

To Brad this serene scene said enough; not wanting to disturb the man's napping, he resolved to execute instantly a hasty retreat.

"Actually what's the hurry? Why should I disturb this sleeping officer, and anger him for no reason?" Involuntarily he recalled the nasty surprises endured last night." It is much wiser for me to sneak nicely out, sit down on the bench by the wall, and wait to be invited in."

But as always, his good intention proved futile. His action turned disastrous, he found himself in a new bind. Exactly on the verge of closing very carefully the door from the outside, a draught alighted God-knows-whence, and slammed the door shut with such a terrible force and bang that the echoes returned painfully in Brad's eardrums many times amplified between the surrounding walls, only to make the poor man's life even more miserable, and overfill his soul with renewed desperation.

"Oh My Dear God, did I sin against You that bad?"

He rolled his eyes several times in the sockets at the same time revolted, resigned, questioning and beseeching. Then, without further hesitation, and without musing on other useless questions, he sat down thoroughly defeated on the bench, as a poor schoolboy caught in the act of mischief.

Too late: from inside came the superintendent's deep, baritone, and typically nasal voice.

"Hey, who is it out there causing this racket?"

Brad momentarily tongue-tied, paralyzed with fear. He could utter not one measly syllable in response. A little later, in the ensuing eerie silence he heard slowly scraping dragged steps on the floor inside, and soon the superintendent's dark figure loomed large in the lit doorframe.

"Ah, it's you." The official's voice turned instantly indifferent, but not altogether unfriendly. "Come on in. Why do you sit out there in the dark?" The man spoke as to an old acquaintance.

Somewhat becalmed, Brad followed the superintendent with sheepish obedience. As the latter approached his desk he closed the door, this time successfully, without any undo noise, but then stayed behind leaning his back against it.

For a long interval nothing stirred in the room, not a single molecule of air. The superintendent, sunk deep in his armchair behind the desk, began to study Brad meticulously, from head to toe, and vice versa. Then as struck by a revelation he slapped his forehead.

"Ah yes, I remember. You must be the freshly arrived fellow the concierge told me about this morning. Hey buddy, everything is fine, no need to be afraid. Come, approach the desk, don't stand there as a pillar of salt." The man spoke benevolently; his forcefully nasal voice did not betray a trace of reproach. Moreover, he seemed quite benignly amused. "See this chair right across my desk? Go ahead, stranger, sit down. Don't be timid, I won't bite, I promise."

Brad noticed for the first time the simple wooden chair his side of the desk.

"How come I didn't see the chair?" he wondered somewhat puzzled, after he sat down, as told. "Well, well, the concierge was right: I am not paying the requisite attention. What the hell is happening to me?"

With this his mind froze, couldn't come up with any explanation. Grown unusually inert, it obstinately refused to find a way out of his enigmatic predicament. Thus brad fixed his gaze on a tinny speck of dirt, spotted slightly off his line of sight on the whitewashed wall between the windows. A strange silence descended in the room that smelled vaguely as dry timber, old paper, and musty dust, all mixed.

Neither did the superintendent show any haste to shatter the quiet interval, and initiate the discussion. Rocking back and forth on his wide armchair, he just kept staring sullenly and insistently at his visitor. A slight dumb smile persisted on his wide bonny mug.

Ever more embarrassed, Brad, the victim pricked by a thousand needles under the seat of his pants, failing to resist any longer, broached the silence compelled once again to push forth his mostly needless excuses.

"You know -, I arrived last night, and late as it was, my body totally exhausted, practically starving, I tried my luck, and knocked at this shelter. It is a shelter, isn't it? Okay, I admit; I don't really know what it is__ anyway sir, please forgive me for disturbing you just a minute ago, when I woke you__ I beg you insistently to overlook my intrusion."

"Ho, ho, ho, ho…" exploded harshly and heavily the superintendent, almost choked in the phlegm rising from the depths of his lungs, until his raspy laughter gradually transformed into a sickly gurgled smoker's cough. "Hey man, do you really think I was sleeping? Ha! Come on now and be serious. Only a dummy can believe such a ridiculously stupid assertion."

The superintendent inserted tinny pauses in between statements and questions – possibly for the sake of emphasis -, and overcharged the words as bad actors frequently do for the desired overwhelming but crude sort of slapstick effect. Then, all of a sudden he regained his earlier gravity, as well as the nasal tone of voice, amplified more than ever, and continued almost didactically.

"In our part of the world citizens do not sleep on duty. Do you hear me?"

Another long pause ensued; only later came the concluding punctuated question.

"Is this now clear to you?" and the superintendent fixed his black, bulging eyes straight into his victim's who forgot even to blink.

Fortunately for Brad the scene didn't last; the superintendent leaned back comfortably in his armchair, and resumed his former good-natured attitude shown to his customer at the very beginning, without passing through any noteworthy gradations.

"If you really must know", he reclaimed his thought, "I have been immersed in my usual morning meditation what to you looked like sleeping, ha, ha, ha. Man, what a misperception! Why would I do such an awful thing? Ho, ho, ho, ha, ha, ha__" the man rocked with laughter, tortured by coughing, choking on phlegm.

Meanwhile Brad went through the entire range of emotions, from awkwardness to shame and anxiety. Finally, naturally resigned to his fate, he grew confident enough to show politely, cautiously a vague tinny smile. But then a new suspicion arose slowly in his mind.

"Could this be an asylum for the insane? How far could my bad luck go?"

On his part, the superintendent paid close attention to his victim. Under the guise of his gushing cheerfulness, he followed Brad's every move, noticed the man's slightest change in demeanor, and watched him for the minutest alteration of expression. Then, without forewarning stopped his laughter cold, and abruptly regained the seriousness of the official engaged in discharging his duty.

Regardless of how alert Brad tried to be, he had been caught again tardy, even if only for a single measly heartbeat, not more. Although the poor man regained quickly a totally submissive, humble and cautious bearing, his face still betrayed traces of the earlier smile. This made him appear to his satisfied tormentor frightened, vexed, and squeezed into enduring another failure.

"Now let us turn the page to serious matters" resumed the superintendent conversing on his usual nasal voice. "You know, my time is precious, and well apportioned. I'm sure other customers might be queuing outside, so how can I help you?"

The official sounded self-important, changing over quite flawlessly from the disparaging way of the boss, or the oppressor's bullying, to the authority's cold and indifferent politeness. He joined his hands, placed carefully his white fat interlocked worm-like fingers on the desk's neatly uncluttered surface, while his countenance showed an expression of well-feigned expectation and good-natured patience.

"As I said, I arrived last night and__" begun Brad timidly, but the superintendent cut him short brutally.

"Very well, very well, this much we learned already." Sharp accents of displeasure and irritation filled his voice, the volume raised a notch above the usual. "Better tell us, where are you coming from?"

"From Rombardia" spit it off Brad quickly and almost inaudibly, as if self evidently ashamed of his origin. By now he adjusted somewhat to answering questions directly, to the point, rather than attempting in vain to recount his story unaided. This approach the wretch employed for reducing the risks of his speaking more than needed, and thus avoiding to place himself in jeopardy.

"Aha. You say you are from Rombardia? Hey, wait a minute. Are you by any chance from the Western provinces?"

"Precisely. That's exactly where I am from, that is from the town of Demlica," blurted off Brad, with a little spark of hope inexplicably lit in his chest.

"Don't say." The superintendent turned friendly again, this time convincingly so. "Small is the world indeed", he concluded and then gazed at his customer, seeming sincerely awed. Soon, the man delved right into his memories:

"In 194_ I've got acquainted to the area, you know, during the occupation. I had been billeted in that town for three weeks or so. Wonderful weeks, I might add. I even recall my address there. It was on Balint Street where I lived at Mrs. Martha Roemer, a very decent mature lady, who rented rooms to foreign army officers. She owned quite a pretty little house under number 68. Say, maybe the house is familiar to you, eh?"

"I am sorry." Brad honestly regretted not knowing the street and the house, consequently felt guilty for it, and launched into excuses. "You know, the city of Demlica is quite large. We lived on the other side of town, on Dr. Shagovitch Street, somewhere beyond the old Orthodox cathedral, if you may recall as much. Anyhow, during the occupation I was a child, and since then many things have changed. But I am sure my grandfather could really enlighten you about Demlica. He loved the city a lot, so he naturally knew it well."

"Is he still alive?"

"Unfortunately not. He perished in the bombardment at the war's end."

"Ah yes, yes. I am honestly sorry." The man expressed his regret mechanically, without any obviously authentic feeling of empathy. On the contrary, he exhibited a grain of irritation, and instantly reverted to his nasal voice, although mellower than usually. "By the way, why are you here in my office now?"

"You know, the concierge sent me, and__"

"Oh yes, yes, you're right. I remember now, do you want a job, isn't it?"

"Sure, I would like to work, at least temporarily. You understand I don't want to be a burden for anyone__ I am a decent honest man, and wouldn't want to get abusive. As a matter of fact, I'd be happy if you tell me how soon I might get an answer to my application? Perhaps you're authorized to inform me, because, you know, I want to cause no undo trouble, and__"

"Okay, okay. But let's take it slowly, issue by issue. There is no need for haste. I'm sure we can eventually help. Just allow me a minute, okay?"

The superintendent opened the desk's top drawer, and took out the file Brad worked on the previous night. Then he sunk deeply into studying the document, meticulously, page by page, completely absorbed in the activity, so much so that to the inexperienced eye he might have appeared asleep.

But the victim had learned his lesson, and knew the man was awake, a state obviously reconfirmed repeatedly by the intermittent turning of pages. So it came as no surprise to him when the superintendent raised the first unfilled page, held it against the light, and after studying it thoroughly, put it neatly back on the desk, only to tap it there three times pointedly with his thick index finger. Finally he shrugged a few times evidently confused, and let out between his teeth some indefinable words, possibly a curse. Following a small pause, peppered with onomatopoeic interjections uttered mostly for his own consumption the official raised his eyebrows, and let out repeatedly some mumblings - "Hmm, hmm"-, then returned his questioning gaze to Brad.

"Well, well, my friend, why did you leave all these pages empty?"

He snatched the page off the desk, and fluttered it before his victim's eyes, as an obviously incontrovertible proof.

"Young man, I'm sure you can offer me some explanation, of what and whys, can't you?"

"Yes, of course I can."

Brad felt wronged. He recalled the previous night, and was on the verge of loosing his composure but, luckily, managed to master himself in the same instant, realizing the precariousness of his situation.

"Last night, while I was filling the forms, I have been overcome by __"

"Fine, fine, let us skip this issue. Actually, I know what happened; the concierge informed me about everything to the smallest details. Anyway, by now is a little late in the game to fix anything. On the other hand, missing a few pages is no big deal, well, not as big as it seems at first. What the heck, we'll have plenty of time for righting wrongs, won't we? The man burst into a loud laughter mixed with coughing, and ended choking in his phlegm, as before.

"Well sir, I can fill the gaps right now, if you wish __"

"To hell with the forms; at this point there isn't really much need for papers. We can manage without, can't we? The official laughed again some, and added. "By the way, your situation appears to me clear enough as it is, without documentation." Then he became suddenly serious, even stern." So, if I understand correctly you intend to go to Newland, isn't it?"

To Brad the question came just in time. It saved the explications, which tortured his fretting soul burdened by too many alternatives the overheated mind tried uselessly weigh with some certainty.

"Yes."His answer couldn't be shorter.

"I could have bet on it," exclaimed the superintendent on the harshest possible tone of voice, after which he feigned absolute indifference, as he leaned back into his armchair pushed onto its two hind legs. "Unfortunately, your case no longer comes under my expertise. I advise you to try next door, at office number 3B, the first on the left to ours, in the hallway outside. After existing, please send in the next customer waiting his turn. Good bye."

His attention totally disengaged, the superintendent gathered Brad's file and thrust it back into the desk's drawer, beneath a large pile. The interview had ended. On his way out, Brad could still see him as he lighted meticulously a long fat cigar.

No one waited in the dark anteroom. Here too, a vague dry timber aroma mixed with perspiration and tobacco smoke lingered in the air. Strangely reassured, the man relaxed.

"So far I've made it unscathed. Let's see what will come next."

He felt exhausted, as having moved boulders. Intent on recovering some of his strength, he sat down on the bench opposite to door number 3B. Soon enough feeling better he decided to try his luck, and knocked on it three short times. A thick familiar voice, answered from inside.

"Come on in."

Brad cracked slowly the door open, and then wished it shut again, thoroughly confused. Behind a similar desk and room, he saw the same superintendent comfortably in his armchair, while delectably puffing on his thick cigar.

"Oh, please excuse me; I must have knocked on the wrong door. Forgive me."

He couldn't believe his senses, to have erred so stupidly.

"She--t, I have to be more careful, much more careful indeed. My situation might be graver than at first appeared."

But the superintendent's hoarse voice interrupted his musings, simply and amusedly.

"Hey man, don't be so impossibly shy. Step in, and shut the damn the door. Don't you feel the draught? How much longer do you want me to wait for your appearance? I had been alerted about your coming. So why don't you sit over here, on the chair before my desk, and let's set to work; we can't spend the whole day just for you."

And to appear more convincing, he encouraged his customer gesturing widely with the cigar, which left in its wake rings of heavy suffocating smoke in the air.

Brad felt like rubbing his eyes, still incredulous. But he needed less than a blink to notice that the room was similar to the former: the same desk, the windows behind it, and the similar portrait between them. Only the door was elsewhere, that is to the right, the warning on it somewhat more specific:

"ENTRANCE PROHIBITED TO FOREIGNERS."

"It's obvious, the rooms communicate," concluded Brad stupidly in a flash, but the superintendent's amused voice quickly denied him to deliberate further on the thought.

"Yes, yes, exactly, the rooms communicate, as you quite perspicaciously noticed." And, as earlier, he burst into laughter, shaken by cough, choking on phlegm. "Yes, yes, and likewise, I am the same person, as you see. Why must this seem so strange to you?"

The man ceased speaking, suddenly preoccupied by puffing repeatedly on his cigar about to go off. Only after securely rekindling it he went on.

"Listen, we are thrifty around here. We must economize. Times are hard; jobs become scarce, companies downsize, cutbacks must be in the offing. To be brief, I have been assigned simultaneously for both jobs. But some formalities must be respected, don't you agree? Well, all these considerations are unimportant, so let us proceed to your case. Information in your file indicates your desire to go in Newland. Is this correct?

The superintendent regained his persona of greatly affected importance, along with the official nasal voice that wiped off the slightest trace of friendliness from his attitude. He grew cold, remote, and more artificial than ever.

"Yes," replied Brad mechanically, seriously wondering whether he wasn't dreaming. He pinched his thigh hard, just to convince himself of the contrary. The response ensued instantly. A sharp pain shot through his body, and produced a grimace the superintendent laying in wait noticed right away.

"Perhaps you are not absolutely convinced yet. Maybe you have second thoughts, and wish to go some place else. At this early stage you may still have the luxury of choice."

"Nah. I've made my decision. It is firm if you don't mind. I insist on my going to Newland. I am quite sure about this."

"Okay. Then so be it. I repeat you are free to choose as you please."

The superintendent leaned back into his armchair.

"Don't be afraid, you're not in anyway obligated to us. You don't have to bend at all to our bidding. The free world is open to you wide, and you are at liberty to go wherever your heart desires. If you wish to go in Newland, so be it. That's your business. No one can stop you. Once again, did you decide to go in Newland?"

"Yes, yes, in Newland."

The victim regained his courage; his voice grew firm.

"Oh well, if this is where we stand, let us jump right to the next step. Before I could send your file to the authorities of Newland, we still have to clarify some minute details. I must remind you that, even though your problem is no longer of our concern, we have some mutual legal obligations to uphold with our partners. Here, on this side of the divide, laws must be abided, you know. So, before we transfer your case to the proper authorities, you'll have to answer a few more questions: why did you leave Rombardia?"

Brad intuited the question and was prepared with the answer, a pretty plausible one, but uncommitted as well. "How could I be certain about the correctness of an honest answer in a world built mostly on lies?"

He often wondered about this paradox during the long preparation time spent before leaving the country.

"I left without giving it much thought__" replied he a short hesitation later almost whispering, his eyes lowered in shame to the floor.

"Hmm," mumbled the superintendent, then leaning forward on the desk opened his eyes wide, and suddenly pointed an index finger to his victim. He subjected Brad to a hard gaze for a prolonged time before formulating the searing conclusion.

"In other words, what you want me to believe is that you left your country unwillingly, and you defected as an idiot?"

"No, I did not say that at all."

Brad's heart sunk in repressed rage. He fell exactly in the much-feared trap. His mind searched feverishly for explanations. However, the superintendent did not allow him the necessary respite, and interrupted brutally with the next question.

"Still, what you seem to say is that nobody forced you to leave. Is this true?"

"Yes. This is the truth, nobody forced me."

The reply sounded curt, exact, simple and definitive. Any change of mind has been foreclosed. From this point on, the runner had to persevere on the road wisely or unwisely chosen. "I must let things follow their natural course," he thought sullenly and obstinately. "I have to keep pushing forward on my predestined way no matter what."

Once over this decision, he gradually calmed down, lowered his eyes again to the floor, and then resolved to study his shoes of an uncertain color and shape.

A grave and persistent silence filled room number 3B.

The superintendent kept his gaze affixed on the man sitting before him, while rhythmically shaking his cigar's ashes over the ashtray littered with foul smelling buts. But he no longer saw the subject of inquiry. His thoughts escaped somewhere far off, lost in the intensity of a situation without exit, into the rarefied space of individual uncertainty, oscillating paradoxically and singularly between the extreme choice of good and bad deeds, extant theoretically far beyond Brad's earthly presence in the room.

"In fact, what the hell do I care about this wretched asylum seeker? Why shouldn't I let him go in God's way, to find his luck with other people in other lands? Nonetheless, as a matter of course, he had to say something to the client in his office, even something trivial, if only for the sake of an appearance rationally tied to the interrogation. Out of the blue he raised his voice and heard himself asking severely.

"Are you married?"

"No"

Brad spit off the denial without lifting his eyes, trying hard to restrain the slight smile about to move his lips. He might have remembered only God-knows-what lately lost opportunities for pairing up with someone he used to love dearly.

"Are you divorced?"

"No, not divorced either."

He felt all of a sudden inexplicably compelled to thrust his gaze right between the superintendent's eyes almost insolently, slightly ironically, absolutely against his will. "You see old man, you wanted to catch me, and you failed."

Naturally our defecting runner held back these thoughts, and outwardly remained mute, unmoved, without even blinking, his face a perfect mask having only a gaze.

Brad's stare at this time turned so penetrating and insistent for the superintendent - until then absolutely on top of his game -, that he lowered his eyes in embarrassment, perhaps in the attempt to hide his evident defeat.

Soon he began fumbling in his cassock's pockets, probably searching for matches. He found a box too, took out a matchstick, stroked it carefully against the raspier, relit his fat cigar, and then, drawing hard several times, blew a few bluish, perfectly foul smelling smoke ringlets in the air. At last, obviously content, the superintendent took the cigar out of his mouth, and after contemplating it with the satisfaction of a thing well done, commenced speaking, this time on the voice of the superior officer discharging his duty.

"As I said it before__ your case is no longer of our competence and - well, it remains to be seen what__" Reaching this point, he changed course, as struck by an idea off the blue. "But tell me friend, why exactly do you wish to go in Newland, and not elsewhere?"

But Brad, now in the lookout, caught the question's insinuating nature, so before uttering his reply, afforded himself a second or two of reflection. He recalled the advice the concierge gave him that he had to avoid by all means erring in any way. "I think I am faced now with a key question, therefore__" but before finishing the thought, a definitely saving idea struck him. At least, this how it appeared to him.

"I wish to go in Newland, exactly for the same reasons everyone else does."

"Ha, but how do you know what everyone else wants? Did you receive some information in this sense, eh?"

The man leaned anew against his armchair's back, while keeping his stare on the victim, extolling the condescending expression of the superior, perfectly aware this time of victory.

Cornered as so often during this uncertain dialogue, Brad relented, and resigned to his fate. Reduced anew to hopelessness, he decided to feign absolute indifference, and abandon himself to chance. This attitude caused him to reply evasively and mechanically, but calmly, only because he had to persist.

"I am quite certain the world is full of things, which even if secret, are nonetheless widely known, especially for people of my kind, __" At this point the man stopped, groping internally for the proper word. In the ensuing pause his mind continued searching feverishly for an acceptable formulation, neutral, inoffensive and as uncommitted as possible, which, lo and behold, he stumbled on, and blurted off before the superintendent could interrupt: "__secrets known to all **tourists**."

Following this verbal explosion Brad relaxed, and breathed easier. The solution seemed adequate.

And true enough, the superintendent pretended to swallow calmly his victim's last outburst of irony and insolence, while looking at him at length with the disdain and cruelty so typical for someone in command. The ensuing earth shattering laughter further emphasized this, accompanied by the eyes' narrowing into slits diabolically slanted towards the temples, where veins seemed ready to burst under the pressure of the man's repressed anger. The howling laughter lasted a lot longer than earlier, with the official leaning deep into his armchair, where he boiled and coughed off phlegm, his face peppery red, and his eyes almost popping out of sockets in the effort.

Brad followed this show a little fearfully, not knowing whether to laugh or stay serious. But then, seeing no end to the amusement, he was about to try a small smile, which froze quickly on his lips, when his interrogator turned abruptly serious and grave. He heard the man's sharp voice striking hard, with barely muted anger.

"You people from **the other side**" - the superintendent disdainfully emphasized the last words -"do you really imagine you can deceive us here, on this side of the fence, ha? It is true and common knowledge that your entire folk are ready to run to Newland. We know this quite well. But we also know dear comrade that you're chasing pipe dreams, whereby you as fairytale knights will ride white horses through rivers of honey flowing on the streets, and catch dogs with pretzels hanging on their tails. Yes, yes, we know this too. My friend dare tell me, am I not right? To hell with you, escaping tourists! I pity you all."

Once finished, the worked-over official had to wipe his forehead with an immaculate handkerchief fished out surprisingly fast from his wide purple red belt tied over his belly. After carefully unfolding the kerchief, he disgustedly spit a large fat greenish slug of phlegm smack in the middle of it. Then apparently satisfied, but still disgusted, the man aimed at his victim a new question.

"So why then have you come our way, when you really wanted to go in Newland, why this unnecessary detour?"

The time arrived at last for Brad to be totally honest.

"Actually, I started out to Gemlonia, where according to some information it is easier to transfer to almost any place. I stumbled to this location by chance. Please forgive my error. Still, let me ask, if you don't mind, presently where exactly am I?"

"For the superintendent the question came just right. He hurried to reply - a visible satisfaction on his face -, and tried to mimic Brad's attitude in a funny way by raising his pitch as high as he could.

"My dear confused **tourist**, I must inform you that you **are** in Gemlonia, exactly where you wanted to get in the first place. My friend, you haven't lost your way at all, as you wanted me to believe. Nobody can get lost coming this way. Do you understand? No one can!"

Brad had been caught short again, and could do nothing but swallow the sarcastic emphasis his tormentor placed on some choice words, such as "**tourist**", "**exactly'** and "**got lost**". Saddened, he lowered his head, unable to utter a single syllable. His mind paralyzed, and only a tiny, tired, barely audible sigh bubbled up from his debased soul.

On his part the superintendent, appearing fatter than ever in his wide, deep armchair, showed eager to go on with his disdainful tirade, while calmly savoring his victory.

"You, my friend, fled your homeland as so many others did before, knowing perfectly well how easy it'll be to go elsewhere from here, for instance in Newland, the place apparently so luring for all you so-called "**tourists**". Most of your ilk seem to hurry in Newland, to the place where allegedly all men's dreams, aspirations and ideals of liberty and prosperity can be quickly fulfilled, only to return later, totally and unduly conceited, just for the sake of looking down on us with the indulgence and contempt of the nouveau rich versus us, people of the old world, out of fashion, modest, and worn. Pfoui! I am absolutely disgusted."

The superintendent shot another huge slug of phlegm in his handkerchief, and fell mute. A short pause later he added.

"You know, I could easily send you back whence you came from." The official's face turned morose, definit bitterness broke through his voice. "But don't worry; we never resort to the procedure, not even with lawbreakers. I am not suggesting you are one. No, not at all." His voice sounded official again, as nasal as could be. "Rest assured that your situation is more than clear for us."

The discourse ended on a tired note, machinelike, dry, in the rhythmical monotony of official decisions.

"I will forward your file as fast as possible to the consular office of Newland."

With this the file slammed closed ended up thrown on top of the pile in the outgoing box, and the superintendent turned around with his chair to face the window, his stare lost at a point beyond nowhere, his back ostentatiously presented to his customer.

Not a single cloud spotted the uncannily unreal and deep blue sky.

"Thank you so much," whispered Brad, for some murky reason simultaneously ashamed and hurt.

"Come on, stop it. Don't thank me. There is no need for that. Go, and God be with you."

By now the official's voice regained a normal tone, and he signaled the interview's end, without turning his gaze back from the window.

Somewhat uncertain, Brad remained glued to the spot - his hands again too long and useless along his thighs. At first he'd been tempted to rush out of the office the fastest he could. But then he felt to say some more. The superintendent, aware of his customer's reluctance to leave, addressed him anew, obviously irritated.

"Man, why the hell don't you get out? Your interview has concluded. It is over. Done with." He suggestively rubbed and slapped his palms together. "Good bye!"

Still, Brad did not budge. Eventually he begun, shy and embarrassed, after uneasily changing the weight on his legs for a few times.

"Sir, if you don't mind, I have a last question."

"Okay, okay, spit it out. But be short, other customers are waiting their turn, you know."

"If you can tell me, approximately how long could the formalities in my case last?"

Brad's question came explosively, in one large breath, the reply slowly, indifferently, and only after long pondering.

"Hell knows how long. Sometime it can last a month, two or three. You know, each with his luck. But why do you ask?"

"Well, I'd like to know where would I sleep and eat during my waiting period."

"Where would you sleep, where would you eat? Ha!"

The superintendent turned finally back to his victim who just stood there glued to the floor, soft but persistent. After sizing him up for a while, two tear drops escaped from the corners of the official's eyes, and rolled down slowly on his fat, wide face.

"As I told you, since your case no longer comes under our jurisdiction, you must address your inquiries to the respective consular office as well. But now I must really bid you good bye."

The official's voice sounded hoarse, hiccups interfered with his last words.

No longer able to find an excuse, Brad had to accept defeat, turned slowly on his heels to exit the room, but not without mumbling a barely audible "thank you". Before closing the door, he heard the superintendent's call again.

"Hey man, wait a second."

Brad froze on the spot, without turning. The official went on.

"Here, keep this temporary food and lodging thicket. It is good for a week." The man held out a plastic card, fished out of the drawer. "When it expires, come back to me, and we'll see what can be done. But now get off my face, and quickly.

Totally confused, surprised for the zillionth time, Brad hesitated. "I wonder what other surprise might hide under this new twist?" he thought while mentally welcoming the card with teary eyes. For no obvious reason the official's sadness infected his soul too. Also he felt the need to say something nice.

"Thank you sir, thank you so much" he managed to say, infused by deep emotion.

He retraced the few steps back to the desk to become the possessor of the small white plastic card, the guaranty of his physical survival for a week, or possibly longer.

Right then and there he realized how simple life could be, as well as trivial, and just how little a man needed for effecting goodness on one side, or satisfaction on the other. His thoughts raced haphazardly, voided of any sense behind his wide luminous forehead. No longer able to figure out a simple way to take leave, and exit the room, Brad still frozen to the spot, repeated stupidly and mechanically:

"Thanks, thanks a lot, thank you __.

Only the official's commanding, but much less irritated voice, coming forgivingly from his comfortable position in the armchair, could move him now.

"Oh come on, and get out of here. What else do you want? Go."

"Mr. Superintendent be not cross, and permit me to ask something else."

"Okay, okay. What's your ache now? Let's hear it. But this must surely be the last thing. Go ahead, blurt it out."

The man seemed completely softened.

Brad hesitated a little then said somewhat hurriedly.

"Mr. Superintendent please tell me, why did you turn so sad just a minute ago? This is important for me."

"That's it. Now you really did it. Get out man, and leave me alone! See, that's how it is when you let the cat in; he jumps right in your place on the sofa. Leave now, double time. Ah, by the way, don't forget; keep running, and never look back!"

Following this advice he stopped shortly, only to continue on the same theme.

"Now listen to me carefully: do not ever stop running. You see we don't enjoy this luxury. Here we can't run anywhere. We do not have the choice, because we are not oppressed, or lost as you people are. Do you understand? Do you? At this point the superintendent frenzied, and switched to yelling, angered and upset.

It was Brad's turn to feel pity, deeply, sincerely but unexplainably for the ravaged official. Next, although longing to comfort the man with soothing words on a soft voice, he could only wonder aloud.

"Is such a thing really possible?" Is it?"

"Yes, yes, it is. As a matter of fact the explanation is simple."

He went on after sighing.

"I, we, cannot go anywhere because we lack the reason to do it. Here in our place everything is just fine and dandy, which for us naturally bars all exits. Can you understand this much? Can you? So get off my face, and stop bothering me with your idiotic questions!"

At this point the official, completely out of his mind, could only gesture his customer to leave the room.

Brad, whether he understood or not, did not wait for a kick in the rear. An inexplicable force reinvigorated his entire being, and he rushed out with lightening speed, surprisingly, without slamming the door. He reached the hall downstairs jumping two-three rungs at a time without hearing the terrible, ear-shattering screeches his haste caused in the old building's staircase. The concierge had barely time to ask him.

"Hey man, slow down. Are you crazy, how did the interview go? What's the rush? Where do you think you're headed?"

"Everything is just fine. Thank you, mister concierge, your advice proved invaluable," replied Brad without halting. Only in the courtyard, where the strong white sunlight blinded him, did he reconsider his attitude. A few steps later, having taken a few deep breaths of fresh, hay-infused air in his lungs, with quivering and dilated nostrils, he felt like yelling his joy towards the sun, when the concierge went on.

"Well, didn't I say the superintendent was in good mood today? You remember as much, don't you?

But the official couldn't yet see why Brad had his arms raised toward the sky, thoroughly flooded with joy.

"What the hell is wrong with him? I did everything in my power to help, and now he doesn't even notice me. Ah, this is man for you, an absolute ingrate," the verdict came, and an innocent, barely audible curse followed: "the son of a bitch_" After turning on his heels, just before reentering, he felt tapped on the shoulder. It was Brad.

"Please forgive me, I was truly overwhelmed. Believe me; I did not intend to ignore you at all."

Impressed by Brad's sudden remorse, the concierge's eyes welled up with tears of joy and gratitude. The flame of hope in man's goodness rekindled in his soul.

"That's okay. Don't worry, I understand. In your place I might have reacted the same way. No harm done." Then, quickly, almost embarrassed by Brad's unending excuses, he added; "Come now, stop the nonsense. Better tell me how did the interview go?"

In the end the man's curiosity, triumphant as always, put an end to the awkward situation.

"It went quite well__ very well indeed, I think. But since we talk, tell me, is the mess hall still open by any chance?"

"Oh, stupid me! Upset because I thought you forgot me, I didn't even ask if you are hungry. It's almost a rule for people just out of the interview to suffer terrible pangs of hunger. I knew about this phenomenon, and still didn't__" At this point he changed course. "Look, do you see the school, that huge white windowless building? But he didn't finish the thought, and slapped his forehead. "Oh my God, is it past eleven o'clock? He glanced inside, at the troublesome clock under the portrait; "Yes, I am afraid the mess hall doors close at nine. My, my, I'm so sorry."

"What do you say good man, no meals are served at this time?" Brad's voice sounded desperate. An instant later he concluded, "Well, I still must go, and try my luck."

That said, he run off in the direction indicated, forgetting the second time about the concierge, who remained glued to the spot, confused, helplessly shrugging his shoulders.

"How to make a hungry man understand objective reality?" whispered the concierge resignedly, spit out a thick fat slug on the gray dusty ground, shrugged once again and went in cursing life between his teeth.

*

A minute later, with no one around, Brad slowed down, and step by step, turned his run into a playful jog. In spite of earlier disappointments, an immense joy invaded his soul, and life seemed suddenly wonderful, promising as the sparkling sun on the spotless azure sky above. A mellow breeze made his nostrils quiver, and an inciting perfume of linden flowers mixed with the aroma of freshly cut hay fired up his imagination, although not a single tree was visible as far as the eye could see at any direction he looked.

Squarely aligned kitchen and flower gardens surrounded perfectly modest houses everywhere in the limitless flat plain, sparsely planted bushes ran along the plot separation lines.

"What a strange village" he mused for the tiniest instant, not yet totally aware of himself and his environment, his mind feverishly absorbed in the morning's events and the promise of a bright future, naturally flowing out of his present situation. A boundless optimism infected his whole being.

Thus he noticed only in passing the bunch of children returning noisily from school. He forgot his encounter with them in the morning, and no longer felt threatened. In his young life, he did not yet endure the innumerable disappointments to learn that an escapee was never offered final peace, and was customarily forbidden strolling in public spaces, open only sporadically and conditionally for intruders.

That much harder was his surprise when he saw the group of children swarming around him, and yelling as skinned alive. Fright contorted their faces as if confronted by a horribly terrifying monster. For these well educated children an alien behaving as a normal, innocent, decent and, after all, peaceful individual could mean only a contradiction of terms.

Wrested off his reverie, brutally awoken to reality, Brad reacted as a compressed spring suddenly released. The muscles of his legs contracted, and re-launched him instantly into the runner's normal rapid and steady stride.

The children calmed down equally fast as to a secret command. They no longer paid attention to the alien, rapidly forgot their earlier hate, and seamlessly resumed their quarrelsome behavior typical for their age; kids perfectly anchored into the present.

"May the devil take these tinny bastards!" squeezed Brad between his teeth a small curse. His heart thumped hard and syncopated against his chest, overheating his already scorched throat. "I hate these savage little urchins."

It took him a while to recover his calm. Only after an appreciable distance covered, and the village safely behind him - the children no longer visible or audible -, and he was still running hard without even thinking to stop.

Thus came the man to his so-called dead point, whereby exhaustion is no longer perceived, and the runner might go on to the end of ends, perhaps right up to the clutches of death. Although his earlier optimism faded to a faint memory, and the dream of a better future evaporated in thin air, strangely enough Brad no longer felt that sad.

But is any man running really sad? Is it not melancholy and sadness by definition a state of meditation? Who can run and meditate at the same time?

When acting against the organism's natural need for comfort and energy conservation as during a run the determinant factor is always volition, which renders impossible for humans to be either cheerful or sad on command. That's why a runner's emotion identified with physical suffering, once it shoots beyond the limit often turns into indifference.

It is exactly what happened to our fugitive. His body pushed to an extreme effort quit feeling pain, his mind ceased to reason coherently. A muddy, gooey, and persistent smear suffocated his thoughts; his soul ceased resonating to inputs, his spirit sank into a bottomless, gloomy and foggy void. Brad kept up his pace as a wound up clock, taking the steady monotonous and everlasting rhythm of running to be his only undeniable internal reality.

And yet, even this state of indifference and numbness had to reach an end sometime. It did, and quite trivially for that.

Out of the blue, hunger and thirst hit anew, this time with such overwhelming force right into the solar plexus, then into the heart, to finally nestle in a strangely powerful vacuum that almost made the fugitive's mind blow up with desperation.

But Brad, the long distance runner he just became, didn't quit. He applied his newfound will in a miraculously superhuman way, and regained his sanity even if just barely.

In vain, because saliva flooded his mouth, and his mind filled with images of food: bread, cheese, bacon, green onions, tomatoes and who knows what other tasty bites. Once again the stomach reclaimed its primordial rights, ignoring willpower, inertia and emotion all at the same time.

Our fugitive had to stop if he didn't want to choke in his own overflowing saliva. Brad did not afford the luxury of choice. The sweet gooey saliva slid down his throat in a large gulp, and it felt almost good. Then, strangely enough, instead of feeling satiated, our man became suddenly terribly thirsty instead.

But for a change, The Lady Luck of that minute appeared to smile on him.

Sunrays sparkled playfully before his eyes on the surface of a pond, probably filled by the rains of yesterday. The water appeared clear, undisturbed. On the bottom of the pond Brad could see tufts of grass, alluringly beckoning in the strong light.

"Huh, a drink of water is exactly what I need. Maybe it could ease a bit my gnawing hunger."

Said and done. The man lowered on his four, to slurp a few gulps, doglike.

The sun-warmed brackish water first tasted good, but as thirst quenched it became fouler and fouler. Then it stank.

He jumped up, shaking in disgust.

"What he hell came over me?" and with these words, uttered slowly and bitterly, the truths of his precarious existence hit him directly in the core of his being. His legs trembled, his heart stood almost still. The future looked grim; didn't promise anything good. Brad fell softly to his knees and lifted his eyes to the sky, prepared to mutter a prayer, or who knows, perhaps a curse against The Almighty.

And then he noticed in front of him two white buildings, reflecting blindingly the light of the sun: the school and the mess hall.

"How come I missed this until now?"

At the same moment he remembered the food thicket the superintendent gave him. He felt saved. After resuming his run, this time toward the buildings, he recapitulated mentally, sequence by sequence, the entire series of the morning's events, intent on figuring some sense amongst them. He had no success. His tired mind couldn't come up with any reasonable or, at least, acceptable answers.

He stopped at the first building, gleaming hot in front of him. Although his gut still protested noisy and angry, an intriguing curiosity came over him. Disbelieving his eyes, he circled the structure several times.

"Why can't I see any doors or windows on the school building?"

Indeed, only straight, flat, contiguous white washed walls seemed to close in the square building under the red roof. The school lacked an entrance and had no windows at all.

"This is weird, extremely weird. I wonder how do the children and teachers enter their classes without doors?" he wondered almost ready to laugh. "I can't even begin imagining the architect who came up with such a crazy idea. Never before could I have believed in the existence of a construction like this," admitted he baffled, but still couldn't laugh. Then he recalled vaguely the Concierge mentioning the windowless school. "It's still hard to accept."

Suddenly his wonder turned off, and Brad felt gripped by a palpably malevolent force the walls emanated, especially those in the shade. Instinctively he turned on his heel, back to safety, towards the sun. It was too late. A shiver of terror ran down his spine. The poor man almost forgot his morning experience with schoolboys and schoolgirls.

A bunch of kids - as noisy, overexcited and threatening as always - appeared only God-knows whence and by what miracle, and was swarming straight at him. Blond and blue-eyed girls and boys, judging by their clean attire, scions of decent families, gesticulated chaotically with stretched out hands, prepared to scratch off the world anything, living or dead in their path.

But then Brad recalled his morning experience, and set quickly to running in earnest. Then the children regained their calm as earlier, and passed by without giving a hoot about the alien.

"What a village, My God where the hell am I?" he exploded yelling as a wounded animal, for the first time aware of a sentiment of futility, of a destiny definitely spoiled in circumstances out of his control, because of one stupid inspiration and demented resolution taken too hastily in the recent past.

"Why did I have to leave my home? Why?"

His outburst, savagely desperate and spontaneous, rolled away far and repeatedly over the open fields, only to reflect in his tortured mind, exhausted body and sickened soul as the ever clearer irretrievable verdict: "How stupid of me!"

Forlorn, with the last glimmer of hope lost, Brad continued running uselessly back and forth, around the school and mess hall buildings, perhaps hundreds of times, a hopelessly broken robot, the inanimate mechanism inertia pushed for ever and ever farther away from home.

He stopped a long-long time later, nearly at sunset, when all around him grew silent - not a single person anywhere in sight.

The black ink of approaching night dripped relentlessly from the universe, the darkness slowly growing deeper, evermore contrasted against the glowing disk of the enormous living sun, about to sink behind the horizon.

Gradually, Brad regained his courage. Now he felt somehow protected under the advancing night's cover, his anxiety pushed in the background by pangs of hunger; reawaken for God-knows-how-many times that day, more painfully and hopelessly as ever. In the struggle between spirit and matter, the latter won again the upper hand.

Then he got a strange reprieve.

The sublime spectacle of nature falling asleep, often stronger in effect than any pleasant or nagging physical need, charmed our hero, and made him temporarily forget the desperation felt just seconds before. The man lost himself into looking awed at the giant reddish sun, as if there, only there, he could distinguish the contour of a promised land.

But daylight was passing, dying by each second, drowned in the ever-faster descending darkness, together with the illusory plans of a dreamer like Brad.

Right there and then the man's body abruptly came to its senses, brought back to a cold unforgiving reality. The sharp, penetrating chill of night suddenly replaced the fantastic show of the setting sun. Instantly Brad knew; the twelfth hour of his salvation chimed. He had to act.

Chill and fear overwhelmed him, as he headed straight to the mess hall's building, so foolishly disregarded until then; he invested all his hopes in the food thicket the superintendent gave him. But another surprise was in store there.

A note - hand-written in large capital letters -, clearly visible in the light of a lantern hung above the door, attracted the famished runner's attention:

THE MESS HALL TEMPORARILY CLOSED FOR RENOVATIONS.

This banal, laconic information filled Brad's glass to the brim with the last drop of the day's disappointments.

He paralyzed, and then lost his mind.

He began pummeling his head with his fists, struggling hard to let off his throat the raging shriek of a man hopelessly lost for the sane world. His face contorted to a lethal spasm, not unlike a wounded animal's last twitch. His mind blacked out, sunk into the absolute vacuity of a lonely existence tethered to absolute helplessness.

Only then could he let off his chest the liberating and triumphant roar of his impotence into the cosmic surrounding silence, and only in the wake of this outburst could he come back to his senses, frightened by his own voice, unknown until then. Brad woke up terrified by his own rage, which echoed far away into the inscrutable dawn of his uncertain future. No one heard him.

"Oh, why didn't I think about this beforehand?" he sighed in resignation, following a few moments of intense listening, and idiotically confused shrugging of his shoulders.

Drained of emotions, absolutely disoriented, Brad became in the end morbidly indifferent, as any human being torture pushed beyond the limits of endurance.

In such a circumstance the only escape is often laughter. Our running man had to laugh if he wanted to live. And he did, in ever more cascading roars provoked randomly whenever he noticed the least significant details of the locked door looming large in front of him. "Ha, ha, ha, ha... hee, hee, hee... ha, ha, ha."

He went on laughing for a long time, until an obviously bright idea hit him out of the blue.

"What if I knock?" Suddenly the solution seemed self-evident, of the purest common sense. "How come it took me so long to see this?"

Said and done. Brad furiously butted his head against the door, and then knocked it with his fists repeatedly as if trying to shake the hinges loose off the jamb. Eventually he even kicked it savagely, but to no avail.

No answer came from inside, not the slightest noise.

And so, after this last unsuccessful attempt, he quit abruptly. Thoroughly defeated, he sat down on the cold step before the entrance, took his head between his palms, his back leaning against the door. Slowly but surly the stone's chill penetrated to the bones, rising mercilessly up his spine. Brad came to the verge of crying.

"That's it, I am finished." His eyes closed, and through some unexplainable psychological process, he recalled a long forgotten day in his life.

Once upon a time, when he was a teenager, he ran away from home in revolt against his parents. At that memorably unpleasant night, the same cold, dark, fear and loneliness tortured his soul.

"This appears to be part of my fate," he muttered softly.

Strangely enough, the idea brought him back to a modicum of tranquility. Minutes later he succumbed to a state of somnolence. Slowly, the chilly sensation melted away, and with it the feeling of solitude. Even silence didn't bother him as much.

But this tranquil state was not to last. Unexpectedly, a distant velvety, vaguely murmured melody hit Brad's eardrums. This perked him up. Eventually he made out a voice, much too real to be just the product of imagination.

Indeed, a few moments later, a small indistinct shape materialized in the dark. A shadow of a man approached slowly, in a well measured pace. Once nearer Brad saw the customary cassock, the typical uniform of officials at this neck of the wood.

"Thank you God" he muttered, and he stood up with hope reanimated in his heart. When the official approached, Brad stretched out his arms, as to a heavenly gift.

"Good evening, mister. I'm so happy to see you."

The official did not reply right away. He stopped singing, to carefully scan the stranger up and down. His attitude betrayed doubt and apprehension. Only then did he open his mouth, speaking as nasally as humanly possible.

"You must be the person who arrived last night, right?"

"That's right. I'm so happy you've heard of me."

Brad strived to be extra polite, even friendly. At this late hour he could no longer afford a gaffe. He remembered his earlier mishaps, and was careful. But hunger and cold persisted, turning him bolder at the same time.

"Tell me good man, what else you know about me?"

"Honestly, not much. Just that I've heard of your arrival. Tell me though good man, why are you on the street at this late and chilly hour of night? For God's sake did no one inform you how dangerous this is? For anyone wandering out of the village, reentry could be forbidden the second time around. Don't you know?"

"Nobody told me any such thing. However I don't believe to have stepped out the village perimeter."

"My, my, very well, very well indeed. You've been lucky" and continued to himself in a muffed, informal tone of voice. "Ha, the bloody bastards never warn the newcomers about this risk" then addressed the wanderer nasally. "So how may I help you, stranger?"

"I'm hungry and cold. Maybe you can provide me with supper and a cot for the night. I don't ask for much, and if you must know, I have a valid meal ticket. I'm not asking for anything illegal."

"To hell with your ticket, it's worthless anyway," retorted the official, and begun chattering his teeth, in the attempt to hold back his laughter. "But even if you swallow the meal ticket, I promise it will not turn off your hunger. You are very lucky to stumble into me. So follow me; I have to feed the chicken before I can help. Come now, don't be bashful, you came to the right place."

By the time the official concluded his invitation he abandoned speaking through his nose. Then he took the lead in a well measured pace toward the backyard of the building.

Brad, given no alternative, followed obediently two steps behind. He felt the man's breath. It reeked of alcohol. "Well, the guy is obviously loaded" he thought, "and this is good."

He remembered his father's long time advice, to always trust drunkards, and avoid people seemingly void of vices. Now he found that man, and his doubts evaporated instantly. "This guy looks surely decent and trustworthy. He is tipsy all right." And from this point on Brad felt an inexplicable empathy toward the man. Even his voice, in retrospect, sounded somehow familiar, less nasal than other officials', although he didn't yet figure out why.

"Chick, chick, chick, chick," he overheard the man's muffled voice calling a bunch of hen, perched up on the branches of a leafless tree, whence they answered back with soft, barely audible, almost musical cooing.

The tipsy man stopped, listened for a short time in obvious rapture, and then proceeded to spread on the ground fistfuls of grains, ladled off the large pockets of his robe. His explanation came a little later.

"Let my little birds have a few tasty pecking first thing they open eyes in the morning. Say, aren't my chicks pretty?"

Although the question was addressed to Brad, the man didn't wait for the answer, and resumed talking sweetly to his hen, "Yes, yes, daddy's little girls, y'all have a good night sleep, my cuties." Only then he turned to his visitor.

"My friend, now let us both get inside." He looked up to the sky. "The night promises to be frosty. Do you see the moon's uncommonly strong glare? This is a sure sign."

"I agree good man. Take the lead."

He did, while the queen of night climbed even higher in the sky. The giant silvery globe gilded the village, the gardens and the fields with a fine greenish, phosphorescent dusting of light, creating a background fit for a fairy tale.

Brad followed his newfound protector in silence. The night's surprising splendor charmed him, almost caused him forget the hunger and cold, if only for a few minutes. Repressed in beauty, his mind kept working feverishly, advising for caution and alertness. Ugly disappointments could still lay in wait. The past day's experience had taught our running man hard lessons.

At the entrance to the mess hall, the official produced a large key off his pocket, unlocked the door, and both stepped into a large room, with rows of long battered tables and benches. Inside lingered the mixed odors of burnt frying oil and stale dishwater. Else, the room was lit, well heated, and silent, precisely what our escapee longed for at the end of his day's exacting turmoil.

The two souls seemed to be the only beings in the building. This the guide confirmed soon, when they stepped into the kitchen through a large double swinging door.

"I am the cook, and spend my nights here when the wife is away from home. She often visits relatives living still in the home village. In her absence I can save some heating oil, which is expensive, you know. Listen, aren't you somehow from Demlica?"

The question fell as a thunderclap off blue sky.

"That's exactly where I am from," replied Brad automatically.

"I knew it," and the man slapped his forehead.

Suddenly his speech turned naturally manly, melodic and soft, all traces of his earlier pretentious twanging erased. His accent became eerily similar to Brad's.

"My ear never lies. I recognized your accent the second you spoke. Be welcomed dear friend. Come on; let's embrace, as our good old custom demands."

The recognition occurred instantly. Both men openly showed their happiness as brothers who thought themselves separated forever.

"By the way, what's your name?"

"Brad Constant." And what's yours?"

"Mihai Destoinic. You can call me Mishu. Can I call you Brad?"

"Of course Mishu."

And the two men embraced the second time.

"My friend, I arrived to this refuge exactly ten years ago. For good or bad I decided to stay, perhaps because I was given this job right from the very start. Later Maria came too. My dreams were down to earth, not about *green horses painted on white walls*. I did not nourish idiotic pipe dreams. Over here in this land life is not fantastic, you know, but is good enough. Then again, we are nearer to home. Later on, you'll see what this means. I bet you."

Brad gazed at his newfound compatriot with teary eyes. He never expected to meet a fellow townsman. But even if he had, the significance of the event wouldn't have hit as hard as in the present circumstance. Moved to tears, he was unable to utter a word, and just kept holding the cook's hand tightly in his, as if never wanting to let go.

"Come man, let us go upstairs. I will treat you kingly. Be assured of that. You may toss your worries aside. At least until tomorrow you'll have no problems. This much I promise. Come dear Brad, follow me."

Then the cook freed himself from the grip of his awestruck co-national, lit a rush-lamp and started forward, leading on the way.

First they went through a narrow, dark corridor with the ceiling so low that both men had to stoop. Their shadows projected large on the damp musty walls, and played chaotically in the rhythm of the dancing torch's flame. The tunnel-like corridor ended at the foot of some stairs, equally narrow, dangerously abrupt, as in a submarine. After climbing to the top, the pair squeezed through a trap door into a dark attic, smelling of fresh pine, unusually warm and welcoming.

"Up here, my friend, we are perfectly safe. Believe me."

The self-proclaimed cook, switched on the light, and then bid his guest by a theatrically large gesture to sit on one of the two chairs at a table, covered with a cloth showing the familiar folkloric black, white and red motives, typical for Romdolva. The room, sparsely furnished, also contained two beds, an armoire, as well as a refrigerator, older than the ages of the two men combined.

"Come Brad, don't be bashful, sit at the table, and feel at home, while I will bring something to eat. We will dine together tonight; we'll drink, and above all else talk. How does this sound to you?

And why would Brad resist, and not welcome such a tender proposal?

Indeed, he began feeling so unbelievably happy he agreed wholeheartedly without giving it a second thought. He sat down as instructed and, not having anything else to do but wait, proceeded to study the modest room, now a safe haven after his multiple misadventures of the day.

On the opposite wall he noticed a window with the shutters down. Through one crack he could see the moon, its sickening cold greenish blue light penetrating between the blades.

"Brrr", he shuddered, jumped up instantly, went to tighten the shutters, and obliterated curtly the strange, unfriendly light, the same that minutes earlier seemed so fairylike, ready to swallow him whole in the chilly night. This time unimpressed, sheltered safely inside, he preferred to forget the recent past.

At his return, the table awaited him set with diverse goodies: coarse, homemade peasant bread, feta cheese, smoked chicken breast, tomatoes, scallions, a large kettle of hot tee, a jug of plum brandy, a large demijohn of new red wine, plates, glasses, cups, utensils.

"Dear Brad, as my fellow villager be at ease and indulge. It's all I have, but I'm sure you'll like it. Don't worry; the food is clean, wholesome and tasty. Guaranteed. All you see on the table is homemade, and I'm proud of it too. Do you remember the hens outside, don't you?" The cook's eyes moistened slightly, but only for a moment, then he winked and concluded in a funny conspiratorial fashion, "Oh well, my poor chicken, God bless their tinny souls, ha, ha, ha."

The guest and his host toasted jiggers of brandy and set to work on the food at hand. For some time only the muffled sound of masticating, the incisors ripping bites of scallion stalks, and the slurping of drinks could be heard in the room. Brad felt in ninth heaven.

But in spite of this overt happiness, the conversation heated up in earnest only after both men downed two or three glasses of wine. This loosened the minds and souls enough for Brad and Mishu to begin slowly unburdening their lives in words, each choosing randomly zillion details amid events that surfaced in memories as the worthiest, tuned to some rules equally impenetrable for the common man, or the savant.

By two o'clock in the morning the new friends found out about each other all they deemed important, mutually enjoyable emotions stirred up in the process of recall. The alcohol accumulated in the blood helped along too. At four in the morning the friends were singing together.

As expected, the first running out of stamina had to be Brad.

Wore down in the day's adventures, softened by the room's coziness, overheated in vapors of alcohol - stomach silenced, finally completely at ease, his eyes closed if only for a heartbeat. The guest's head fell to his chest - a cigarette hanging between his lips. The drooping head awakened the tired man for an instant, but he quickly relapsed, but not before reflexively squashing the cigarette in the ashtray.

Mishu the cook, more at home in his own environment, naturally less challenged than his fellow townsman, noticed his new friend's struggle to stay awake, and decided gently to put an end to the nocturnal bash.

"Hey, my good friend Brad it's time to quit. The bed over there is nice and soft. Let me help you to it. Would you allow me?"

"Yes, yes, I will, but only if you promise no to get angry."

"Now why would I do that, my dear? Look, I can sit by the bed, and still chat with you a little. Agreed?"

Brad acquiesced by bobbing slowly his head twice. Then the cook helped him lay down, covered him carefully with the quilt, and gently caressed Brad's forehead with his calloused hand toughened through hard work. He kept at it until Brad closed eyes. Then he got up, turned the light off, and stretched out on the other bed.

Soon the rhythmic breathing of the two men filled the room. A few hours earlier the mutually unknown souls, suddenly found themselves tied together with strong, but invisibly thin threads.

In the peaceful night Brad dreamed.

"He was at home, running on the main street, skillfully leading his steel circle with a properly shaped wire on the sidewalk of reddish bricks, under the shade of well rounded mulberry tree line with freshly white-washed trunks. While running he amused himself trying to crush with his rolling circle the thick white or black berries fallen to the ground, paying attention not to squash any with his bare feet. He reached the corner exactly in front of the grocery store, where he always used to halt for catching his breath in the air filled by sweet aromas of coffee and vanilla emanating from inside.

Next sequence he moved to the sunny side of the same street, running this time under the blooming acacia trees that swarmed with busy bees collecting fragrantly sweet honey. The atmosphere was filled with buzz and intense activity.

Giving in to temptation he stopped and reached to pluck a bunch of the white soft flowers. Then - with the steel circle set on a shoulder - he headed for home happy, greedily biting big chunks off the sugary bunch of challises.

In front of the familiar forged-iron gate he halted to finish his improvised snack, to throw his circle over the gate and jump after it.

He never burdened himself with the keys. On the other side he advanced along the alee running between the building and a long line of evergreen hedge, turned the corner to the left only to jump lightly over the three steps, leading up to the entrance. Once inside the hall, he dutifully paid attention to the crack in the old floor, complaining noisily under his weight.

His mother, stepfather and younger brother Victor waited for his arrival. They were sitting at the dinner table in the kitchen. Brad realized his dire situation on the spot.

As always, he was tardy.

He took his seat and sunk his head in meek humbleness, prepared to listen contrite to what was surely to follow; the same zillion-times-warmed-up, old questions the humorless stepfather addressed him with stern monotony, and his mother interrupted often and loudly with desperate yells, to the joy of the always well behaved younger half brother, who barely could hold his stifled and malicious sneer or grin.

"May we know why you are late to dinner?"

Not a word out of Brad's mouth.

"Now why don't you answer?"

Still not a peep.

"Young man, look at your mother. Don't you see how worried is she? Don't you care for her feelings at all?"

Continued silence.

Brad continued mute and obstinate, pretending to study his plate gaping under his face as a round hole he could happily plunge in if possible, to disappear there perhaps forever

"Yes, yes, my son, why don't you look at me? Be so damn good and show me your eyes. I want you to see the tears I'm shedding on your behalf. Hey boy, look at me! Do you really want to kill me?"

The mother's voice sounded heartrendingly admonishing and melodramatically sad.

But little boy Brad remained obstinately silent.

"I asked where you have been?" intervened the stepfather annoyed, his impatience barely kept in check.

"I haven't been anywhere."

"Oh, yes? I'll teach you, dastardly rascal, to answer me like that. Hey momma, where's that belt? Nothing else works with this stupid boy of yours."

"Hey Johnny, forget it. Save your nerves. You know how this affects your liver," turned the mother the tense situation around, then to the boy.

"As for you, __ march to your room! Today you will stay hungry. Get up, and go! Now!"

Stepfather John was breathing heavy, his spectacles about to fall off his nose. He could barely restrain his fury, though in the end he managed to keep his composure, and stick to his seat.

Brad got up prepared to obey his mother's orders, as so many times before. Right then and there the saving idea hit him out of the blue.

"I will have to run away. I can no longer endure life in this house."

He turned on his heel and ran out of the house, into the strong light, off to freedom.

He found himself on the street.

He had grown up, and was a young man. At the corner the policeman stopped him.

"Hey, comrade citizen, what's the hurry?

"I want to cross the street."

"I'm sorry, it is prohibited."

"Why am I not allowed to get to the other side?"

"Simply because I say so; that's why it's not allowed. And now since you know the reason, please behave, and turn back," ordered the policeman, and raised his baton, showing the clear intention to hit Brad in the soft of his head had he not obeyed."

In the same second Brad awoke panting, drenched in sweat.

Calm, peace and darkness filled the room. Only the rhythmic, reassuring breathing of the sleeping cook disturbed the silence.

Unseen, unheard, a perfectly lonely person in the new world, the runner looked up to the vaguely perceptible ceiling. He grew sad, and muttered what he saw written on it.

"From now on, my friend Brad, you will have to live by small installments, one day to the next."

He promptly fell asleep, this time deeply and voided of dreams.

WASTED STRUGGLE.
(or Failure)

Costa opened his eyes, and saw the rich brilliant light streaming in through the window. As so many times, he forgot his dream promptly. Then the alarm clock rang, and definitely destroyed the last evanescent rags of Orpheus' world, so real only moments earlier.

Angered, disappointed by the failure, Costa chewed a tinny curse between his teeth, and got out of bed to head for the bathroom. He had, as yesterday, as the day before yesterday, as all mornings, to face another day without the oracular benefit of dreams in which he believed blindly.

A former repairs department chief at the streetcar depot in the city of Timisoara, Romania, and presently head waiter at the "Wandering Vallah" restaurant in the posh suburb of Bethesda, North of Washington, Costa Jordan learned from people versed in the occult sciences that when a person wakes up with eyes facing the window open to light, all dreams will be instantly forgotten.

Absolutely convinced of this fact repeatedly confirmed with his own dreams, he tried desperately through diverse concentration techniques performed before bedtime to wake in the morning facing the wall, not the window. But all proved useless. He never succeeded although struggled a long time for it, beginning perhaps as long as two years ago, after divorcing and moving hermit-like into in a cheap suburban apartment, quite a distance to the restaurant. Yet, it never occurred to him that light might have caused his failure, and not the window, so easy to obturate with thick black drapes.

A deep sigh and a long empty stare later, Costa began soaping his deeply wrinkled face for the daily shave, looking in the mirror above the dirty bathroom sink. In the lemony light of the lone dusty light bulb dangling precariously at the end of two dangerously worn wires on the wall above, sadly purplish edemas underlined his eyes, contrasted glumly to the white foam. In the semitransparent shadow, thick bushy eyebrows cast a shadow over the man's melancholy eyes, causing his bottomless black, enlarged pupils grow even larger.

A specific exhaustion, the invariable result of a monotonous daily routine, the boredom of an unimaginative life lived day by day, nested nagging in his body regularly intoxicated by smoke, alcohol, coffee and junk food. This unmistakably showed on his face as well.

Costa's age pushed a little over fifty years. Lately his headaches became more frequent, especially in the mornings, as it happened that day. But he never complained. Living a lonely life, he had no one to confess his troubles either.

His friends and the few acquaintances anchored in his life's port simultaneously with his wife's vessel twenty-five or more years ago in the refugee camp in Traiskirchen, Austria, all abandoned him soon after the divorce.

Their children, a daughter and a son, flew off the home nest long ago, visited him rarely, and then mostly asking for money.

Every now and then, Costa considered seeing a doctor, perhaps undergo some blood tests, to prevent more serious trouble had something proven wrong with him. Unfortunately such rational decisions never materialized, never turned into actions. On the contrary, the man avoided with equal fervor doctors and actions as the devil fears frankincense, thus his decisions ended up much too frequently suspended somewhere between nothing and everything, in one word, in limbo. Unfortunately, incorrigibly stubborn as he was no one ever proved able to change him either.

Then again he was used to being healthy. Hardly any ills ever bothered him seriously, and he could not imagine the situation to change out of the blue. Common to people of his kind, he believed himself to be indestructible.

Moreover he didn't avoid doctors without reason. Costa hated doctors so badly as to consider them useful only for the sick, not for the healthy, the man sound in body and mind he fancied to be.

"I don't see why I must place my neck voluntarily in the noose," he calmed his conscience repeatedly. "Doctors are mostly good for suggesting you ill, for turning your life miserable with their accursed admonishing and practices. Isn't this the way doctors earn their living? Of course, was I to get a warning in my dream; it would be altogether different, totally different. But thanks to God, I haven't received any such warning yet." Thus Costa's turned consistently a blind eye to the alarm signals his body gave lately ever more frequently.

No wonder then, that several minutes later - face polished by the blade, body invigorated in the shower's cold stream, and mouth freshened by the toothpaste's menthol - he sat down to the breakfast table in the kitchen, prepared to enjoy the daily hot aromatic coffee and the day's first cigarette, oblivious to all ominous signs his face and body showed him earlier in the mirror.

And, lo and behold, his headache melted away. Life suddenly and miraculously appeared less vapid.

He turned on the radio for news. More than anything, Costa was waiting for the traffic reports, which theoretically armed him against getting stuck on the road later, an effort frequently useless given the increasing daily clutter on the streets of modern cities, in his view, yesterday's engineers habitually mismanaged, thinking rather as horse-riders than car-drivers.

But, by and large, our character didn't pay excessive attention to such trifling questions. His mind kept engaged mostly for remembering last night's dream, whence he expected beautifully palpable images to surface any minute; some symbolic information surely charged with significance.

Unfortunately this didn't happen today, or ever.

Nonetheless, Costa arrived at the restaurant in his usual frame of mind, centered on his obsession. He didn't register much during the hour and a half spent on the road, neither the severe accident on the beltway, nor the police cars or the ambulances converged on the scene, as usually rather to obstruct than allow the traffic flow.

That week Costa had to be on duty in the morning, for breakfast and lunchtime, a schedule he preferred because it ended early in the afternoon. Even so, he complained often, more so wintertime, when he had to wake up in the dark, long before the morning sleep's last dream-world episode.

"So what's a man in my position to do? This appears to be my lot, peppered with good and bad at the same time", pondered he wisely as he stepped boldly but absentminded into the dinning hall.

"Hey Costa Grecoman, good morning", greeted him in a choir his colleagues, exclusively Romanians – waiters, waitresses, busboys, the barman, even Nick Demetrescu, his friend and boss –, as he marched amongst them flaunting a severe face and a stiff body all the way to the dressing room.

"Good mo'ning guys, good mo'ning."

Costa returned the greeting politely but, as always, the nickname deeply affected him, seeing it as stupid and totally senseless.

"I really wonder when my idiotic colleagues will get tired of this charade. Anyway, what's the connection between me and Greece, or a Greek?"

He pondered this annoying question even in the dressing room, while unfolding his uniform, pedantically taken out of the locker.

In a way he was right. Costa had been born Romanian; not a trace of Greek blood flowed through his veins. He saw light first in Brăila, a city on the Danube with a sizable Greek minority, but, but…. his folk came from the Olt River's left bank, where – some say - people speak the purest Romanian.

This fact alone made him enormously proud, almost as if he was single-handedly responsible for it as his own accomplishment.

From Brăila his parents moved to Timişoara soon after the war. In the city Costa grew up in the company of Banat Romanians, in no way with Greeks. Thusly the nickname rubbed him absolutely the wrong way, insultingly so.

To his colleagues he often expressed his dissatisfaction reproachfully, even in protest.

"Please good people, stop calling me El Greco. I am as Romanian as you are. One day the nickname might anger me badly, and then—"

But the reproaches and protests caused no echo whatsoever, passing unregistered by his colleagues' ears. They continued using the nickname, amused on the account of their colleague's comic annoyance.

"Hello Costa El Greco, how are you? Hey Costa the Greek, why don't you help me? Costa of Greece, do you care to share a glass of wine with us?" and so on, and so forth.

Freshly out of the dressing room, the boss stopped him on the narrow corridor leading to the dinning hall. A stranger accompanied him. Costa never saw the man before, a middle aged, tall, quite handsome and well-dressed stranger, exuding a distinctly aloof, almost distant demeanor.

"Come Greco; let me introduce you to Mr. Militant, our new maître d'. Today is his first day on the job with us. We hired him yesterday. The others made his acquaintance earlier."

"Costa Jordan," introduced himself emphatically, and then extending his hand he swallowed hard the bitter knot unpleasantly stuck in his throat. "So I had been railroaded again. There is nothing left for me other than finding another job. I won't stand a chance of advancement in this damned place," he thought, but outwardly kept the dumb polite smile on his mug.

"I am glad to know you. Welcome in our midst," continued he aloud, feigning an additional false, needless exuberance.

Feeling a little cowardly on the account of his reluctance to show any dissatisfaction, his mind came up promptly with a proper justification for the unbecoming friendliness just showed; "Well, I am wronged all right, but is this reason enough not to behave within norms of civilized behavior? I don't think so."

His wounded pride had been saved.

The newcomer must have sensed something gone awry, because he accepted Costa's hand politely but firmly, and responded in a clear, cool, almost stern voice.

"Aurel Militant. The pleasure is mine. Nick had only good things to say about you. We will work well together. I honestly hope so."

"Yes Greco my friend, I spoke to Mr. Militant about you. I told him about your valuable contribution to the success of our business, which might not even exist without it. Being a member of the founding group, I also mentioned the size of your share in the business. Be assured of it."

"Yes, of course you told him all that" mimicked Costa the boss in his mind, "but you hired him, not me, in spite of your many promises. Yes, yes, I know, we need new blood - as you say - because we're no longer young. It is better for us old-timers to withdraw in the shadows. Yes, I am well aware of all that crap."

All of a sudden Costa's face dimmed and his heart sunk into the deepest mud of bitterness. But Nick the boss continued indifferently, without suspecting any of his friend's inner turmoil.

"And now that you're acquainted, I leave the two of you alone. Mr. Militant, please inform him about our new plans, and the possible changes we contemplate in the restaurant. Please Costa; listen carefully and patiently to his ideas. I find them quite interesting. Surely you will too."

Nick the boss concluded his introduction, and retreated tactically and politely to his office, leaving the newly acquainted guys to themselves, strangely bathed in the cold, unnatural neon light, flooding the corridor from behind matted glass plates in the ceiling. These lights flickered vaguely, as did the two men's thoughts wander aimlessly for a few seconds in the wake of the chief's disappearance.

It was the new maître d' who broke the uneasy silence first, and addressed his new subordinate a simple question calmly but firmly, using the tone typical for the superior in rank.

"Mr. Jordan, I wish you can spare a few minutes, can't you?" but the man's words sounded rather as a command then a question. Costa clearly sensed the difference.

"Yes, yes, of course I can. On Tuesdays business is slow."

"I am happy to hear that from you. It's exactly what I want to discuss. Please, let us step into my office."

Then the new maître'd ordered two cups of coffee from a waitress who happened to be nearby, opened the door, and coaxed his subordinate in with an overly large, theatrical gesture.

Costa knew the modest room well, both as the storage room, and as the records office. He often dreamed about the damned place becoming his own one-day, partly because it shared a common wall with Nick's' room. Around it the poor man nurtured secret plans for the future, although never done much about them.

In all honesty the enclosure deserved much better the designation of the storage dump it plainly was than the office it masqueraded for. The shelves filled with staples of all kind – potato and flour bags, cooking oil containers, mustard, tomato paste jars, and boxes of spices and other premixed powders, so on and so forth, all products needed for operating a restaurant – left little space to accommodate the metallic table and the two rickety gray chairs, dumped there who knows whence, when and why. The unmistakably pungent smell of raw onions competing for primacy in their different stages of fermentation became immediately evident to the intruder at opening the room's door.

But Costa loved the dump. Such trifling details as foul odors never bothered him seriously. Since the former maître'd quit, he imagined himself in this room. Once the switch will have occurred, he planned to introduce some order in it.

"Why would I need a larger office?" he fantasized. With a little elbow grease anyplace can be made fast nice and comfortable. Man sanctifies the abode isn't' it?"

In advance of his being named the new maitre d' he bought a polished bronze plaque, and engraved it with nice, elegantly cursive letters -, "Costa Jordan, Maître d'hotel" - exactly as he did for Nick before the restaurant's opening.

"What, as a serious shareholder don't I deserve as much?" argued he alone. "Why shouldn't I have my title on a plaque affixed on the door of my office?"

This time he wasn't lying to himself. He possessed ten percent of the stock, significantly more than the others, each with only six percent.

Costa brushed gallantly aside the fact that Nick detained the majority of sixty percent that gave him the sole decisive voice in the business. But why dwell on such insignificant details? Why should an honest and devoted friend of Nick look at reality from such a cold, objective, maybe even envious angle?

Can then anybody be surprised at the terrible confusion the strange morning's events caused in Costa's mind? Wasn't the poor soul justified to feel as a negligible entity, a partner treated as a nullity, obviously less valued than the intruding newcomer - on top of it -, hired to be his superior?

"Okay, okay, I must stay reasonable, and act within the limits of decency, at least for now. However, I will have to talk to Nick, ask him what the hell happened? I am sure, there must be an error somewhere," argued he mutely, as he took his seat to face the new maître d', who sat across him at the improvised desk.

Then Costa almost forgot the new maitre d', although he kept an empty gaze on the guy, who pretended to putting a little order on the desktop crushed under piles of open or closed files, sharp or dull pencils, large and small paper clips, two old-fashion ink blots near a telephone set, all distributed randomly around a large, square scheduling calendar, scribbled top to bottom with random notes.

"Well, the man obviously tries hard to appear busy on purpose. Evidently, he doesn't know where to begin. Nick must have told him about my privileged position in the business. Anyway, let him find his level of comfort. I have plenty patience."

Thus pondered our character, while under a guise of studied indifference he carefully eyed every move the new maître d' made. Instinctively he wished to figure out his adversary's character, and adopt the right attitude vis-à-vis him from the very start.

Well, the subordinate deciphered his superior well enough, but not entirely. Indeed, the new maître d' allowed himself some thinking interval, not because he felt ill at ease, but rather for he wanted to line up his ideas, contemplating to talk to his subordinate clearly, succinctly to the point, intent on establishing a good first communication bridge between them. Eventually he had to work with Costa. Why not seduce him, lure him to his side the soonest possible?

Nick listed to him the restaurant's problems, informed him about the almost exclusively Romanian clientele, and the profit they brought, much lower than expected from Bethesda's sophisticated and wealthy public. The boss also warned him about the personnel's, but especially about Costa's stubborn resistance to change.

The new maitre d', with a rich managerial experience under his belt, gained in fine, large restaurants, was swayed precisely by this attitude of his new boss, when he accepted the position. He concocted grand plans for improving the service, as well as the choice on the menu, for restructuring the personnel, extending business hours, and other smaller suggestions for increasing efficiency and maximizing profits.

But for now, careful not to create the wrong impression right from the start, he decided to proceed cautiously. Therefore he broached the conversation with an invitation.

"Mister Costa, if you don't mind I propose to address each other on a first name bases. I guess the age difference between us is negligible, so let's place formalities aside. What do you say?"

Unprepared for this approach, denied the luxury of weighing it carefully, Costa agreed reflexively:

"Of course, of course, why not do that? You're quite right."

He fell into the trap. The one setting the rules had been Aurel Militant, not Costa Jordan.

Realizing instantly this handicap, the latter added with a short, forced laughter.

"Oh, yes, yes, Mr. a, a, a, a-a-a" - he was desperately trying to recall the man's name – "you're right."

"Aurel Costa, Aurel is my name", helped out promptly the man. "But for my immediate friends I am Aurică, as you are Greco for yours. Am I correct Greco? I overheard the men calling you this way."

The new maître d' didn't realize the gaffe he made, how wrong he rubbed his new subordinate. How could he know what the damned nickname meant for the man, especially off a newcomer's mouth?

But Costa, true to his nature, didn't have the gall to correct Aurel. He timidly swallowed the nickname as another secret offence, leaving his adversary ignorant, to continue unaware in his error." I better not to let him know about my personal problems. His ignorance might even work to my advantage" reasoned Costa secretly with the slyness typical for the coward, and accepted the man's friendly invitation, and tried another shrill laughter. He launched into a new useless explanation, with a hint of sarcasm

"It's true; my simpleton colleagues call me Greco, although only God know why. Fortunately I've grown to accept the nickname as a term of **endearment**. "

However the mâitre'd proved perspicacious enough, and readily caught the nuance of ambiguity in Costa's statement. "Oh dear, dear man, if the nickname bothers you, I must quit calling you so. I have no intention to hurt your feelings and__"

"Forget it boss, I beg your pardon, Aurel. You should call me as all the colleagues do. Why make an exception with you? It would be senseless, wouldn't it?"

"Okay, then **Greco**. I hope everything's fine." The man over emphasized the nickname, and laughed conspiratorially. "For a second I believed you didn't like the nickname. But if I was too hasty with the proposal of my friendship, forget it. Really, I mean it."

"Oh, come on, A--, A--, A-- ... Aurel."

Costa didn't feel at all comfortable with his boss on a first name basis, especially when it had been imposed on him, so to speak. Nonetheless, he added:

"Generally I am not bothered by such trifles as an idiotic nickname and__"

"How right you are my friend. Do you smoke?" changed course the maître d' tactically, probably suspecting Costa to still withhold something.

Realizing the difficult and ultra-sensitive person he had to deal with, the mâitre'd quietly changed gears: "I will have to proceed more gingerly." He recalled Nick's warning in this sense, and offered his pack of Marlboro over the table.

"Unfortunately I do smoke, too. Thanks."

Costa extracted a cigarette, and began searching his pockets for the lighter. He found it quickly enough to extend the light ingratiatingly to his new boss, who by then had the cigarette between his lips.

"Huh, look at this poor soul hoping to seduce me with a cigarette; two points for me, zero for him. Now I won the game. He is definitely mine," whispered Costa in himself, savoring a tinny satisfaction, which the pleasure of the first smoke in the lungs might have caused more than his secretly enjoyed victory.

Soon in the puny little room the fine bluish tobacco smoke strangely mixed with the fermented onion stench, forming an altogether unpleasant combination, intriguing but hard to describe.

The atmosphere between the two men finally warned up, became more conducive for a good discussion. A few cigarette puffs later the new maitre d' broke the silence.

"You might wonder why I want to speak to you. Here it is; I need to get acquainted with the personnel to learn everyone's opinion about our business. The rest of our colleagues already spoke their minds. Now it's your turn. I am happy to hear you out too, perhaps more so than the others, less important shareholders."

Aurel avoided on purpose using Costa's nickname, wanting to confirm or infirm his earlier suspicions. But his interlocutor didn't betray any conflicted emotion. He seemed calm, self-assured, a person of consequence with unshakeable convictions.

"Ah, our business works quite well. We have a steady clientele, totally satisfied with our tasty dishes, the pleasant atmosphere and the quality service we provide. "

Costa blurted off his evaluation in one breath, his chest properly inflated with pride, his tone betraying the awareness of a man who evidently contributed to this success.

"Exactly. It's precisely the subject I need to address, our profit, which, forgive me, I consider stagnant if not worse. Isn't profit supposed to increase constantly? I hope you agree with me on that."

This new twist surprised Costa. It even annoyed him. For several seconds he felt lost, didn't know how to react, what to reply. He resolved to proceed carefully and thoughtfully.

"Hmm. I don't know whether I agree or not. After all, everyone is a winner here; we enjoy our roles, personnel and clientele, fellow Romanians acting together. Why should we wish for more? I really don't see what could be better than doing a good job such as this."

"My, my, how can you say such a thing? Whoever is not progressing is really regressing. In business, my friend, it is almost sinful to be content with what you have. Life doesn't favor those just treading water."

Indignant at Costa's opinion, Aurel jumped up gesticulating widely, and paced back and forth a few steps in the narrow space behind the table as a caged animal.

From the businessman's vantage the maitre d' did not exaggerate at all. He made sense.

At the "Wandering Vallah" the clientele consisted mostly of Romanians - neither numerous or rich – of the émigré community of Washington and its suburbs. They patronized the place generally on weekends, on weekdays preferring their home cooking, as they used to back in the old country. In the restaurant this loud bunch enjoyed a good time, spent as little money as possible, and failed to bring in the fantastic profits Mr. Aurel Militant dreamed about.

According to him, only the indigene clientele could bring in significant profits, Americans wealthy enough for expressing their boundless curiosity, unquestioned urge for generosity, need for comfort, love of expediency and desire for luxury, all at the same time. Only they possessed enough money to be transferred unquestioningly into the pockets of émigrés nestled amongst them.

The Chinese, Italians and Greeks had learned the lesson long time ago. Armed with this knowledge these immigrants opened restaurants, carryouts, or other food establishments in the tiniest American cities and towns. In these establishments the born Americans spend money to the emigrants' benefit, unlike Romanians, Hungarians or other smaller ethnic groups, who often redistribute wealth amongst them, out of one pocket into to the next, without enriching at all their own communities.

This was the subject Aurel Militant wanted to discuss, prepared to monologue on it, and explain in detail to his subordinate the making of a prosperous affair, adjusted to the dictates of a global and diversified economic environment

But he had to stop short, when he glanced at Costa, and saw him desperately searching for an ashtray in order to avoid shaking off his cigarette's ash on the floor. Seeing these futile efforts, Aurel suddenly felt an unexplainable pity for his subordinate.

Just as well, for Costa, tortured by infinitely lesser concerns than the restaurant's success, no longer paid attention to the maitre d'. Petty and awkward, caught in the grip of a trivial obsession of not adding a little extra dirt to the never swept, gray cement floor in the miserable pantry or office, he got totally distracted.

Taken off his track, Aurel shuffled through the clutter piled on the table, and at last managed to find a terribly bit-up, cheep aluminum ashtray. In the process of fishing for it he uncovered a small penknife - hilts made of a strange pinkish-red plastic material.

"Here, hold on to this, and forgive my impoliteness," and Aurel handed the ashtray to Costa, pondering whether to resume or not his argumentation.

"Thank you, thank you, you're very kind."

Costa accepted the salvation promptly, even gleefully, relieved to have avoided spilling ash on the floor, and finally able to squish his cigarette in an ashtray. "Well, this is how I am, perhaps a bit too civilized." The thought flashed through his mind, when his eyes met Aurel's slightly puzzled gaze."

A few small coughs later, he straightened against the chair's back, hoping to hide the embarrassment, and go back to the conversation interrupted earlier. Next second he paled, his body paralyzed, as the penknife inadvertently exposed amid the clutter came in his focus.

All of a sudden the image of this rather smallish penknife stole Costa's attention away from everything else in the room, from Aurel, the room, the business, their discussion. With eyes bulging he could see nothing but the accursed thing.

Old memories flooded his mind; blood rushed into his cheeks, strong emotion filled his soul. A strange motion picture commenced rolling fantastically fast behind his forehead, bringing back to life events that occurred some twenty-five years in the past.

"Costa felt transported to the old country, where he had been working as an engineer at the streetcar depot. He was busy doing nothing special, other than shooting the breeze and dillydallying in the tool repair shop, together with the night shift foreman Mircea, his high school buddy, and a talented jack-of-all-trades. For these precise reasons he hired the man to work directly under his supervision. They enjoyed being together, more so during the nights of low demand, when the streetcars needed little attention.

Besides, the friends could use the shop's tools for their own little projects, as for fabricating all sorts of metallic objects out of scraps: scissors, knives, peculiar looking penknives and daggers with diversely ornate hilts, at times garbage pails or, exceptionally, even commercially hard to find replacement parts for automobiles or motorcycles, theirs or their friend's. But more than anything they loved to manufacture decorative penknives out of forged lamellar steel spring, the best in flexibility and hardness, thus ideal for blades.

Following a long experience, the two succeeded in producing true works of artisanship, such as the penknife Aurel uncovered. These peculiar looking switchblades fitted with red plastic hilts, were to be engraved and presented to friends and acquaintances. Soon the penknives became so famous and prized in town that the *artists* marked them with their fused initials: MC, from Mircea and Costa.

This obvious success made the friends increasingly popular, as their creations ended up in the pockets of many proud citizens of Timisoara. And when the artisans grew aware of their fame, they did not shy off some loud bragging that grew to exaggeration, especially amongst buddies, sharing on occasions one too many a glass of wine."

The memories flooded Costa's soul with warm pleasure.

But then, the poor man fell abruptly back to reality, his gaze still affixed on the damned penknife, shooting demonically tempting glimmers from atop the pile of junk.

This penknife arrived in the New World safely tucked in Costa's pocket. He never parted with it before presenting it to his friend Nick, at the "Wandering Vallach" restaurant's festive opening ceremony, held a few years back. The gesture was meant to portend good auguries for the just opened business' success, and as a token of supreme generosity and friendship, reaffirmed with the occasion.

And lo and behold, this unique penknife, so wholeheartedly presented to a dear friend, lay neglected on the desk of a stranger, misplaced and mishandled precisely as Costa felt that exact time.

The warmth of his memory melted away fast, not unlike the white drop of milk he poured that morning routinely in his black coffee.

Then it happened. His chest heaved, and a sharp excruciating pain burrowed smack in the center of his heart he all of a sudden ached to touch. Blood drained fast and visibly off the veins in his temples and cheeks, trying to squeeze through the jugular narrows, then penetrate lower, to warm, if only by a measly degree, the ice nestled in the disturbed ticker. A sickly shadow came over Costa's face to render it instantly into a mask of death.

Aurel witnessed the scene helpless, not knowing what to believe, or say. Never before did he witness anyone exhibiting such a strange behavior. It did not take too long for the tense situation to make the maitre'd truly uneasy, honestly worried. The man responded instinctively attuned to the emotional sequencing typical for any sane person, when confronted with the suffering of a fellow human being.

"Hey Greco" - the man tried joking –, "what's wrong with you? You turned to the color of this wall. Do you feel ill?"

To Costa the nickname sounded weirdly similar as the bell might do for the boxer about to be knocked out. However this saved him. The peculiar nerve the nickname painfully pricked proved electrifying. This hurt brought the poor man back to life from the clutches of death.

"No, it's nothing." He mumbled something barely intelligible.

"Everything is fine." "Only you are so annoying," but he never sputtered out loud the last part. Instead he said, "I must have a slight indisposition, nothing serious."

Costa took great pains to underline the manner of addressing the maitre' d, making it his choice form of protest against the friendly but patronizing insolence of the new boss.

"No, no, I am all right. Mr. Aurel, nothing is wrong!"

He raised his voice, became aware of it, and then lowered it to a whisper, to add almost as an afterthought:

"Maybe you're right. I feel a little nauseous, and my head aches a bit."

"Hey buddy, I'm sorry. We can postpone this discussion. The world will not come to an end because of this. But wait a minute; I have some aspirin, why don't you take a couple. Maybe it'll help."

Aurel reached in his pocket and took out a vial of "Bayer" aspirin.

"Here, take these tablets with a full glass of water, then go out for a walk in the fresh air. Don't worry about a thing. Our problems can wait. What do you say?"

"Oh no, I'm sorry. Please, forget what I said. Really, my head isn't hurting that bad. The pain will probably subside soon, as it so often does. It happens to me sometime__ Perhaps I smoked too much; then again, it is so hot in this crowded room."

At this point the man stopped talking.

His gaze fell back on the penknife, obsessively fixated on the blinding shimmers of light the blade playfully reflected. In Costa's mind the re-ignited passion of disappointment overheated, a siren begun whining sadly, painfully alluring, and the ship of sanity snapped its moorings to sail off reason's safe harbor, out on the wide see of uncertainty.

Henceforth his words came out burbled mechanically, monotonously robot-like.

"I will open the window," and without waiting for approval Aurel did exactly that.

The street's noise – the uninterrupted whir of tires on the asphalt, the screeching brakes, the loud yells of workers unloading merchandise - suddenly invaded the room.

Out in the city life bubbled indifferent to the insignificant personal worries of its citizens.

How could the large, rough city, spiced with diversity, feel the sweet sadness of a single spoonful of honey melted in the bitter hot tea of a single cup of human sorrow, as it empties in the gutters? But then again, why should a tinny individual's sigh be heard in the vastness of cosmic space?

"You feel better now? I hope the noise is not too bothersome."

"Oh no, not at all, I am used to it," Costa retorted still absent, his mind gone far, far away to happier times. Spellbound, and through God-knows-what-twist of memory, the open blade's alluring shimmer transported him back again to a peculiar scene in his youth.

<They were just streaming out of school, scattered in small groups, adolescent boys walking coolly cowboy-like, perhaps in poor imitation of a John Wayne gait. Cigarettes hung between their lips. Obviously they imagined themselves older than they were; trying to project a sense of power and independence, some say, for the benefit of the few adult passersby, on their turn annoyed by the children's puffed up, boisterous behavior.

In truth the boys wanted to impress only the bunch of girls approaching from the opposite direction. Amongst the girls was

Cornelia, a lanky missy, better developed than the rest, a gal who enjoyed teasing Costa, just to convey her liking him.

The boy, although happy to see the maiden, behaved often awkwardly, bashfully, and at times ridiculously trying to hide his embarrassment through some clowning, ruefully performed for her amusement. He must have done it well too, because the girl signaled her pleasure by issuing several sensually charged little shrieks and yelps.

The language of the first sexual attraction set to work inexorably, mutually understood, perfectly fit in the ancestral mold, perhaps more innocently on her side than on his, as the proper etiquette for their age demanded.

This happened at the same time the infamous hoodlum Goanţă, the neighborhood bully, made his appearance on the scene, surrounded by his subordinate younger cohorts under his command. These miscreants relished terrorizing their fellow teenagers, humiliating them in front of their girlfriends.

Costa grew in time wise enough for avoiding such encounters cautiously and skillfully, but at the time he found the strategy difficult to employ in the presence of Cornelia. He couldn't afford such wisdom without appearing cowardly in the girl's eyes, he taught. Thus he had no choice other than staring destiny in the eye, regardless of his inner apprehensions.

He tightened as a compressed spring. A big knot formed in his gut, his fingers involuntarily closed into fists, while his mind raced between myriad alternatives.

The parties came face to face; two roosters prepared to fight – so-to-speak – to the *death*. As Costa expected, Goanţă made his move first, and opened the trial pretty sure of himself - the well-versed goon he was.

'My, my, my, isn't the guy in my face Costa the nerd, who all too often skips paying his tribute?' Then turning halfway to his group of little buddies, asked, 'Hey kids, am I right, or what? He, he, he.'

The hoodlum hissing as a snake, slightly but humiliatingly touched Costa's nose tip, an aggressive gesture executed with his index finger.

Costa stood his ground, resisting the attack without budging an inch. Then choking with repressed fear and furry combined, he uttered through clenched teeth.

'Listen Goanţă, and listen well; why don't you turn nicely on your heels, and walk away, this time without causing any trouble. Please. Can you do this much?'

But Goanţă wasn't in a generous mood. On the contrary, hearing Costa's impossibly insolent request, he burst into a hysterical laughter, only to stop abruptly and thrust his mug into Costa's - his fist prepared to hit hard the moment his victim stepped back instinctively.

But nothing of the sort happened. Costa held his ground. This took Goanţă by surprise, made him momentarily relent, and turn lazily to his subordinates, to deliver didactically a lecture on the new situation, on the next proper measure to be applied.

'You see my kids what bravery our friend Costa can suddenly show us? He wishes nothing more or less for me than to execute a one-eighty, and mind my own business. Well, well, why ain't I nice for once? Look Costa, I oblige.'

And he did, just to illustrate the point, prepared to deliver his blow the next instant.

But the threatened boy, now on the lookout, suspected the move. Under the pressure of the imminent shame to be inflicted on him before Cornelia's very eyes, he succeeded in acting quicker, and administered a well-placed kick in Goanţă's derriere, before the hoodlum knew what happened.

The right-foot-kick proved so hard, that Goanta almost lost his balance. Totally surprised, momentarily startled and shaken in his self-respect, he gave way to his first instinct, and ran away, the bunch of kids in his wake.

Equally surprised by his own reckless deed, Costa turned pale as a ghost, trembling slightly - a reed in the wind. Then realizing his triumph, he quickly regained a well-affected dignity, walked away sporting a cowboy like gait, and left Cornelia behind without addressing the baffled girl another word. He felt redeemed. >

At this point Costa fell off his reverie straight into the stark reality of the small, chaotic storage room, the office of the new Maitre d' as well. It was the latter who put an end to this daydreaming.

"Hey Costa is anything wrong? If you wish, we can postpone our discussion for some other time. Maybe you should go home, and take a rest. What do you say?"

"Oh no, I definitely won't go. No way. I am on duty. Let's have our business discussion right now. This is why we met, isn't it?"

"Yes of course. Still, let me tell you, this is not urgent. There'll be plenty of time for that. I'm sure; the opportunity will come up sometimes again. But now you look ill, and I suggest you go home, or see a doctor. However, the decision is up to you; I wouldn't dare to impose__ well then, as you wish."

A first Costa acquiesced, nodded and got to his feet, but then hesitated and didn't budge an inch. The damned penknife's blade still sent maddening shimmers in his eyes. His gaze froze on it as a disoriented rabbit in the high beam of an oncoming car.

The maitre d', believing his mission concluded, turned his attention elsewhere, and proceeded to shuffle things mechanically on the desk, hoping to gloss over the uneasy silence created between them. He gave his subordinate a decent time for retreat, striving to avoid further complications.

His well-intended tactic failed miserably. Fumbling amid the disorder on the desk, he noticed the bloody penknife; picked it up, prepared to switch it shut, and simply throw it into the drawer He had to stop in midair, frozen on the spot at hearing Costa's desperate, heartrending cry.

"No-o-o-o! Don't do that!"

The man raged, eyes blood-shot, ready to burst off orbits.

"Don't touch that blade. A-a-a__ please put it back on the desk. I beg you sir, drop the knife."

The convincingly insane outburst upset anew Aurel's self-assuredness. Costa's shocking, impermissible reaction made him obey instinctively. Dumbfounded, he let the knife drop and withdrew his hand slowly. This sort of behavior called for prudence. 'From here on I must proceed carefully'

A second later the maitre'd turned gingerly towards his subordinate, still raging across the table. Bits of foam leaked through the man's lips.

"My, my, Greco, you must be seriously ill. Why don't you go home, and__?

Aurel inadvertently poured gasoline on fire.

"It's nothing wrong with me, mister!" broke in Costa, all of a sudden incredibly stern. "You hear? I demand, I beg you firmly you call me Mr. Costa. Greco is not my name. Let me prove it."

He took out in rapid succession his wallet, off it his driver's license.

"Look! Please read it aloud!"

He handed Aurel the laminated piece of plastic.

"Yes, yes Mr. Costa, let's stop the nonsense. Please forgive me; I meant no offence__ there is no need to show me your license. I'm really sorry."

Aurel walked over to Costa, took him gently by his shoulders, trying to sooth him and nudge him towards the door.

"No problem Mr. Costa, please go home now. We'll talk later. I promise. Once again forgive me, and don't worry about a thing. Okay?"

"Okay, okay, I'm going."

Costa grew limp exactly as unexpectedly as his rage caught fire earlier. He fell back to his natural mold of timid passivity. But now, on top of it, he trembled shaken spasmodically as he struggled awkwardly to replace his license in the wallet.

"Mr. Aurel, please believe me I am not Greek. Really, I am not at all Greek. God knows why the nickname stuck. I see no reason."

"Of course Mr. Costa, You're not Greek. No one's Greek in this place, I know. My mistake, please forgive me."

At this juncture the maitre d' stumbled. No longer sure of his approach, he tried hard to avoid a new scene.

"Dear Lord, why is it so hard to deal with people?" he sighed behind Costa's back, and silently lifted his eyes to the ceiling, while attempting to push him gingerly out of the room, to get rid of him somehow, but to no avail.

The situation kept tensing up. Costa resisted, didn't show any willingness to leave the room. He stubbornly anchored himself to the chair's back. A moment later he buckled on the spot, and sank on the seat as a large bag of soft mud.

"Mr. Aurel, please allow me to sit?" whispered he barely audible.

"Of course Mr. Costa, why not; sit right there."

The maitre d' acquiesced, prepared to accommodate the man's any wish, only to avoid further trouble.

To be more convincing he even helped Costa gently up against the chair's back.

"Thank you, Aurel."

Costa relaxed indeed a bit, although his eyes remained trained at the penknife, on the table.

Silence descended in the miserable room. Both men fell in their thoughts; the maitre d' desperately searching for an escape, his subordinate for self-control definitely lost in the ambiguous circumstance.

It took a long time for the ice to brake. Finally Costa did it; a new trip into remembrance transfigured his visage.

"Mr. Aurel, can you spare a few more minutes?"

"Sure I do. I have all the time in the world."

"Okay. Then allow me to tell the story of my maternal grandfather. May I?"

Derailed in all his intentions, surprised again by the unexpected turn, annoyed and intrigued by the impenetrable enigma of his subordinate still visibly concentrated on the penknife, the maitre d' gave his consent instantly.

"It will be my pleasure, Mr. Costa. Go ahead."

"My grandfather Vasile, my mother's father, was a sailor."

"What a coincidence, mine too worked in the navy, you know, on the Danube."

"Ah, Mr. Aurel, the fluvial navy doesn't really live up to its name. Everyone knows that. Anyway, that's irrelevant, so let me go on__"

At this point Costa's uncertainty dispersed visibly, as the morning mist evaporates in the summer sunlight. He looked firmly intent on telling his grandfather's story calmly, without undo embellishments.

"As I said, my grandpa Vasile served in the blue navy, and crisscrossed the world's oceans several times. Later the old man often recounted his fantastic seafaring adventures to me, to his wide-eyed young nephew. Naturally, I absorbed grandpa's tales, my chest swelled with pride."

For a minute, grandpa Vasile seemed to loom great anew in his now adult nephew's fired up imagination.

"At the fluvial navy, eh?" he exclaimed dismissingly. "No real sailors serve in the fluvial navy. No way mister maitre d'!

At last the penknife forgotten, Costa noticed Aurel's apprehensive posture, of a man carefully withdrawn into his own shell. This made him feel strong, superior. The boss' resigned attitude made him regain full confidence.

"Yes, my grandfather had been an authentic sailor. No, what do I say? He had been a pirate. Dou you hear Mr. Aurel? **A true pirate!**"

This affirmation Costa emphasized on a strangely emotion-charged voice.

"Can you imagine Mr. Aurel, what it means to be a pirate, eh? Can you? I guess not."

Mmmm, aaaa, to be honest, yes—no-- I can't -, not really. Well, I've seen movies, I red books__"

Fresh, new doubts lit up in Aurel's mind: "What if this guy is out of his mind? Maybe he lost his faculties."

However, he continued listening to Costa's story superficially; interjecting here and there vaguely approving words, while feverishly looking for a way out of the jam, perhaps of danger."

"Huh, movies, books! All those are just fictions, nothing more. Listen, grandpa was real, the real McCoy, a true pirate. Do you believe me, Mr. Aurel, don't you?"

From here on Costa addressed his boss in all imaginable ways, ranging from extreme politeness to topmost familiarity, often imbued with sarcasm, then infused with doubts, or even with veiled threats.

The maitre d' perceived these nuances increasingly worried. Gradually fear got his best. Afraid of nastier surprises, he watched Costa carefully, looking for the slightest signs of trouble in his subordinate's fluctuating behavior.

"Ah, and what a pirate my grandfather was!" boomed Costa at one point, and leaned across the table, as if reaching for the damned penknife.

"Yes of course, sure he was a pirate, Mr. Costa no question about it. Please stay calm, no need to get upset__"

"Come, come, Mr. Aurel, I'm not at all upset. Why would I be upset? Nothing like that!" he thundered, jumped to his feet, bent far across the table, but still couldn't grab the accursed knife, just a few inches off his reach.

Across the table, Aurel watched and couldn't figure out what to do. Whatever he tried with the guy nothing worked. He was prepared even for a desperate move; to knock on the wall, and yell for the coffee he ordered, which, inexplicably, hasn't been yet delivered. Then a new surprise stopped him in his tracks.

Costa slumped back against the chair's back; his stare lost straight ahead, glacially piercing into the deep void. Obviously, he floated away, instantly transported into another realm. Miraculously, unexpectedly, a scene lit up vividly in his memory, the dream he so annoyingly forgot in the morning.

<He was soaring above the vast sea, tracing large circles on the sky. Down bellow moved little boats, white sails inflated in the wind. Pure nirvana. Then out of nowhere a hideous crow appeared, and brought this unbelievably silky happiness to an abrupt end. Petrified in terror Costa begun falling for sure to crash into the waves, growing ever larger, clearer and nearer. But the impact never came. Only darkness ensued. >

"What could be the meaning of this?" he wondered the instant he landed back into the storage room with the maitre d' sitting across the table. Unusually aware of himself and his whereabouts, he met Aurel's worried stare.

Pale and mute, frozen stiff into his seat, the maitre d' was about to burn his fingers with the cigarette, entirely turned to hot ash. Costa noticed it, and politely handed over the desk the ashtray he used earlier.

"Here, Mr. Aurel."

"Thank you."

"Mr. Aurel, perhaps you're right, and we better postpone our talk for some other time. It looks like you are not up to it either today. Goodbye."

He got up, clearly putting an end to the meeting. Aurel felt relieved. But before finishing a deep sigh, Costa stopped on the threshold.

"By the way, Mr. Aurel, please hand me the penknife with the red handles, you know, the one before you on the desk."

"What knife? What knife?"

Instantly, in the men's mind the earlier suspicions revived full force.

"You know, the penknife lying on the pile of papers."

Costa's tone sounded matter of fact, white, lacking any nuance.

"It's yours?"

"Not really, well yes. It's a long story. Please, hand it to me."

"Costa, why don't I give it to you later? Now is not the best time."

Obviously Aurel tried a last, desperate shirk.

"No. I must have it right now."

Costa's sudden calm and self-control frightened the maitre d' even worse than his earlier craziness. "Too many unexpected changes occur in this man's behavior. I better not hand him the knife" he reckoned, "or if I do, at least I must switch the blade shut."

"Costa, allow me to take a look at the knife first. May I?"

"Of course, why not?"

Aurel picked up the knife and inspected it carefully. Two engraved initials and an inscription were clearly visible on the hilt: "**CM: in the memory of our friendship.**"

"What do the initials stand for?"

"That's another story. I might tell it to you sometimes. Well, why not now? Look—"and Costa recounted the penknife's history, and how he presented it to his friend Nick, at the restaurant's opening night.

Soon the tension between the two men evaporated, the emotional storm on both sides subsided to complete tranquility. The unexpected confession and its acceptance opened the gate for a relaxed communication apparently so well shut until then. Costa concluded his story simply.

"And now you can see yourself, the penknife is rightfully mine. Wouldn't you say so, Mr. Aurel?"

"You convinced me. Here, take it" and the maitre d', thoroughly relieved, handed Costa the knife.

Costa took the knife overcome with emotion.

"I thank you very, very much."

Visibly moved, he caressed the shinny object with a tenderness and love, usually reserved for the living, not inanimate things. Slowly and carefully he switched the blade open, lifted it in the light, to enjoy with teary eyes the shimmer of the finely polished steel.

"Isn't spring steel the best for forging knife blades, Mr. Aurel?"

But the maitre d' understood little about steel, so just shook his shoulders in excusable confusion. Obviously the quality of metals didn't impress him much. All he wanted was to get rid of the man, to see Costa off his office. Traces of suspicion persisted in his soul, worries sure to be revived for the tinniest reasons.

It still took him by surprise when, Costa moved the knife in his hand with lightening speed to his heart, only to fall on his knees, then on the floor, his body crumpled, face contorted in pain.

Now truly terrified, Aurel came to the rescue as fast he could, but not before the man's eyes turned icy, and foam re-appeared between his bloodless lips. At first Aurel thought the poor guy committed suicide. Soon he learned that something else happened, equally serious.

Costa, his body frozen on the floor in a final spasm, was still clutching the damned knife to his heart. Through the man's death rattle the maitre d' could only guess a few senseless words, some vague babbling.

"The crow__ I'm crashing__" and the body stiffened on the spot.

It looked like poor Costa expired on a last soft sigh cut short. The waitress with cups of coffee on a tray busted in just then.

Aurel jumped up jolted by her shriek. He almost ran her over as he bolted off to get help in a hurry. He bumped into Nick the owner, who appeared in the doorway, behind him the entire morning crew, motivated by curiosity and empathy for the fallen colleague.

"Somebody call for an ambulance!" yelled the owner, leaning over Costa to check the man's carotid arteries. "I feel his pulse. It is slow, but it's there."

Minutes later, seeming like hours for the people gathered around the body on the floor, the ambulance arrived. Costa had been carried off quickly on the mobile gurney, the penknife still clutched spasmodically to his chest.

The following morning, the boss reported the news to the assembled crew. Costa survived a severe heart attack that required a triple bypass surgery. Whether his faculties got afflicted, was as yet unclear.

*

A few moths later the restaurant changed its name. From the *'Wandering Vallach'* it became *'Le Vagabond'*. Gradually the clientele changed too; Native Americans replaced the majority of Romanians. In the dining room English became the *lingua franca*, and sophisticated international dishes sporting French accents predominated on the menu. Only two Romanian specialties were retained, the *'mititei'* and the *'baba ganoush'*, the first without garlic, the last without onion, just like that, to keep the breath of new customers odorless.

Following his surgery and recovery, no one saw Costa around Washington anymore. Soon everybody forgot him, waiters, friends, even his own son and daughter. For a while the rumor was he returned to Romania.

If true, there he finally might have achieved the freedom he longed for; to catch dreams in the frame of windows open to a word finally his own, and amid his own folk. Some say he was given the new nickname of Costică, a soul reborn among men and women strong as evergreens, and allegedly smarter than anyone in the infinite Universe.□

MEEK AMID BULLIES.

(or In the Dusk.)

In Potzleinsdorf the city appears mostly asleep.

To the visitor wandering into this "village" - a select and aristocratic suburb in the "*achzehten Bezirk*" in northwest Vienna -, whether arriving in the morning, at noon, or at midnight, the narrow streets paved with time-polished basalt stone would always appear sunk in deep silence.

In this veritable "*faubourg*", neighboring "*Potzleinsdorfer Schlosspark*", in late spring the older houses run over by patina and ivy try modestly to hide in deep courtyards amid luxuriant vegetation.

In contrast, the new houses peddle their wares to the street, exhibiting proudly and enticingly modern architectural forms, cut usually in white marble slabs that only the never open windows of vivid colors cheer up.

Both the newer and the older houses to the newcomer might seem abandoned, the inhabitants departed in who-knows-what places, in vacation or on business.

Cars seldom roll on these streets.

Pedestrians walk even less often, then mostly old men or women, probably pensioners climbing up the hill slowly from downtown, perhaps to find relaxation in the park, sometimes to feed the wild, noisy, hungry geese, eager for the unexpected tidbits thrown for them in this serene landscape frozen in time.

In this picturesque neighborhood, in a sumptuous villa showing time-corroded plaster on the walls was located by who-knows-what-whim of chance the branch office of an American telecommunication firm.

One employee, the American Radu Șerban Milescu - of Romanian extraction -, a proud descendant of an old Moldavian family that modernity's democratic upsurge had wiped long ago into insignificance -, was dispatched here in Vienna with the mission to bring to completion the last details of a project undertaken in cooperation with a local company.

*

"I was to take off next morning, homebound to Washington DC" - began Radu his story, repeated to the smallest detail among friends for the umpteenth time -, "so I lingered in my office long past regular hours, having to finish my activity report.

Gradually it turned dark. A mellow spring evening was about to descend above the old city. Through the open window of my office on the first floor, the park wafted in freely its cool mysteriously scented fresh fragrance. The profound cobalt blue of the spotless sky above created an equally strong impression as it flooded the room with eerie, dim light.

The clock on the wall showed a few minutes past nine, when I gathered my papers into the briefcase that I clicked shot, then turned off the lights and exited the office, feeling good about my day's work.

Walking through the long corridor, I became strangely aware of my exhaustion. The deep silence combined with the night shadows, sticking in semi obscurity to barely distinguishable furniture forms, sharpened my self-awareness even more. In this state of mind I reached the corridor's end without bumping into anything. Watching my steps I continued down the stairs to the lower hallway. Under the light of a weak, dust-covered service bulb, sculpted ornaments barely showed their shapes against the strong desk-lamp glare persisting on my retina as a green, slowly vanishing spot. I also remember how the large spiraled wooden staircase screeched, protesting under my hesitant, well-measured steps.

That peculiar night, ignoring all the critters living in the walls, I must have been the only being alive in the old villa that surely had seen better days in the past. The present day's neglect had to appear obvious to any keen observer through the wear and tear of the beautiful details, carved above the walls everywhere in walnut, ebony and other noble essences.

Indeed, the building had a strange history.

The first aristocratic owners abandoned it soon after its erecting; first to some insignificant department of the Austrian state; then to Gestapo Headquarters during the *Anschluss*; after the war to the Red Army's Officer's club; in the end, following many insipid owners, to the branch office of the American telecommunication firm.

Neither the indifferent Austrian bureaucrats, nor the henchmen of the German military police, or the scions of the Russian revolution - rough soldiers steeped in egalitarianism -, properly appreciated the sophisticated beauty of this grand dame of a building, designed to the esthetic requirements and for the refined enjoyment of the by-gone imperial high bourgeoisie.

The Americans, paragons of practicality and simple efficiency, naturally immunized against the beauty of the, so-to-speak, rotting creations of the Old World, showed a similar disrespect for the villa, cluttering its rooms and corridors with the whole gamut of high-tech machinery, necessary to modernity.

But let me return to my story.

As I said, I held on tight to the polished banister while counting my steps. At the twenty-fifth I felt under my foot the first floor plank's inert solidity, at the same time when the screeching protest of the staircase subsided to the lesser noise of the worn mosaic parquet. A right turn later I walked in the vestibule.

Through the dimly lit glass rectangles of the entrance door that filtered in the twilight's soft shimmer, I saw the so-called light at the end of the tunnel. I felt saved. Now the only thing was to aim straight ahead toward the light, turn the knob, step out, and pull the door shut behind me. Six steps lower, in the anteroom I had to repeat the moves, then in the yard traverse the short tree-lined alee up to the forged iron gate, and go out on the sidewalk, on the deserted street sunk in the bluish-green haze of the early moonlit night.

Across the street, the motionless park caught in the web of an eerie silence sent the humid wafts of its tree crowns' large, dark, common mass of uncertainty over the houses and things, as if wanting to muffle any twinkling of life under the open Universe above.

Lost in the infinite space, immersed hopelessly in the deceptive and a bit ominous charm of darkness, first I decided brashly to confront it, and foolishly pierce its secret veil. I, the little insignificant bug of a man squashed into my lonely existence, tried to defy the Grand Cosmos.

The reprimand came deservedly at the next heartbeat in the form of an icy shiver running down my spine, as a lightning's myriad volts would flow instantly through a metal rod into the ground.

And what else could I have done, but humbly bundle tighter in my coat and hurry down the hill, pursued by the syncopated sounds of my own steps, echoing between the houses, repeated as well in my conscience as phantoms of imagination?

Far away, perhaps a little over a mile, I could see the soft twinkling of the few lights surrounding the terminus streetcar station.

Second by second I've grown used to darkness, which seemed less and less dense after each step. The brisk walk warmed up my body, and slowly melted away earlier uncertainties. Soon my imagination focused on the delicate Wiener schnitzel and the proper *trocken*[1] wine, awaiting me in some good restaurant downtown. The thought charged my body with renewed energy, and the need to satisfy my thirst and hunger, underlining the frailty of my soul no longer preoccupied by insoluble problems.

But I kept alert as the street's details ran chaotically by me at great speed. Feeling a tad lonely and vaguely apprehensive, my senses stayed acutely alive, just as my spirit wanted it during those uniquely fantastic minutes. Free to enjoy the mystery of dusk at will I meditated over random thoughts the eternally moving impressions caused on my retinas, eardrums, even on my skin.

Then unbelievably, in spite of my rapid strides, at a certain point in time I no longer felt to advance at all. The rhythm of my walking slowed, almost grinding to a halt.

---

1   dry in German

A strange melody came to life lugubriously in the background; my self-awareness melted irresistibly into the Universe above, whence I greedily absorbed thousands bits of information, just barely acknowledged.

Miraculously, I found myself on the verge of living through that rare moment seldom given to humans, when the lucky chosen individual bursts off the enveloping space cocoon to learn in an eye blink more wisdom than philosophy lectures can provide in years.

Unfortunately, this privilege was not reserved for me that night, or ever after.

I deeply regret the loss, because I am quite convinced that right then I was about to receive my flash of revelation, so crucial for the spiritual health of any lucid human spirit. I am convinced that precisely during such uniquely unforgettable moments the individual begets the requisite gift of his later happiness, to be recorded in the cosmic memory's eternal bank as the choicest of exotic flowers.

Too bad! The unexpected promptly, punctually, miserably and fatally prevented my illumination as always.

Lost on the deserted street, mulling over my near meltdown in the wonderful Universal Infinite, gradually I became aware of some dragging steps, first barely audible, then clearer as they approached behind me.

The onset of this new reality chased definitely away my incredible cosmic reverie, and instantly replaced it with acute apprehension, with a palpable sense of worry.

Now-a-days such a feeling normally arises in any decent citizen's conscience, partly induced by the sensationalism of the contemporary media, constantly pouring fear and uncertainty over the stressed minds of people living in metropolitan environments almost anywhere in the world.

All of a sudden the nightfall's unique beauty and softness melted away, the unreal glitter of stars ceased, even the velvety coolness of the breeze turned to a chill.

Luckily for me, the earlier wonderful sensations - so freely and innocently available to young children – had time to record in memory, and be added, even if shattered, to the collection of my few lone meditative moments as an adult.

But the next moment, I could no longer hear anything besides the muffled sounds of soft leather shoes dragged on the asphalt, rhythmically and predictably interrupted by another man's rigid stride and thump typical for the lame.

My apprehension proved correct. Soon I could hear the men's voices, which my imagination attributed quickly to some overly unpleasant persons, speaking a malefic but strangely familiar language. I understood all the words a couple of apparently mature men uttered distinctly as they engaged in a most bizarre, threatening dialogue.

One guy's higher pitched voice, hissed not unlike the British actor Michael Cane's, the other voice brawled lower and harsher, bringing to mind the famous movie star Peter Ustinov, of Russian extraction. At some surrealistic level, the first character spoke with a suitable Cockney accent, while the other man betrayed his origin as a Russian, both obviously on purpose.

Then I felt their hot heavy breath on the nape of my neck, as they continued to brag boisterously and nonchalantly about their deeds, vividly describing their heinous, unspeakable crimes allegedly committed earlier in the park.

'So, what do you say my buddy Justinian, wasn't' I swift when I cut the little prick's throat, ha? Did you notice how he couldn't utter a single syllable before expiring? Please say that you agree; I've been mighty impressive, haven't I?'

'Yeah, yeah, that's right, you were quite impressive,' retorted Michael Cane's resemblance called Justinian, on his familiarly sullen, but sharply metallic voice.

'And what do you have to say about the man's wife, as the wretched stupid woman implored me to spare her life?'

'So what do you want to hear me say, my dear Kolya?'

'Oh, come on Justy; please try to be a bit more generous with your praise. Don't tell me you I didn't awe you with the speed I cut open the woman's jugulars in one swift swish of my blade. Please don't say that the blood squirting out of her throat as from an artesian fountain did not faze you. I want to hear nothing like that.'

'Okay, okay. I must admit you finished off the woman with a truly masterful slash. What else do you want me to add to this?'

'And what about the infant?'

'What's with the child?'

'What's with the child? I want you to admire and acknowledge the gentleness and humanness of my approach. You surely witnessed the delicate manner I lifted the little bumpkin, terrified speechless by the murder of his parents in front of his very eyes. You saw how gently I soothed him, and wiped his tears – a tragic situation, wouldn't you say? Then wasn't it superb when I fatally stabbed the little guy with one skillful blow applied through his ear, directly into the brain, just to save the poor kid from any useless suffering? Didn't that impress you at all, my buddy Justinian?'

'Okay you win, I was impressed.'

'So that's it, I was impressed? You can come up with nothing fancier?'

Peter Ustinov's likeness called Kolya mimicked his friend in comic exasperation.

'Can't you add anything, some garnish, some extra praise, the expression of unbound admiration or, at least, a little formal encouragement? No my friend Justy, this won't do. No, no, and no.'

Now that I learned my characters' names, they became really terrifying, exploding to huge proportions in my imagination.

Inexplicably, I recalled my high school buddy, strangely named Justinian, who used to threaten me with his large physical presence, and annoy me with his voice, quite similar to the actor's. The resemblance of the voice to my childhood enemy's shook me to the bone. The uncanny coincidence seemed absolutely astonishing.

But I didn't have time to ponder on it long enough, when Justinian intervened promptly, calmly and tersely as before.

'Forgive me Kolya, right this minute I'm not in a chatty mood.'

Then the two hoodlums - Justinian and Kolya - kept walking in silence, as for me, dumbfounded by what I heard, I wandered; what was the chance for such an impossibly strange likeness between two random individuals? Practically zero. And there they were: Kolya as Peter Ustinov, and Justinian as Michael Cane.

My mind overheated, almost short-circuited in the attempt to focus on the enigma, surprisingly and miraculously woven through a harmless reverie the charm of late spring twilight induced. Then my sense of reality got totally skewed, garbled and entangled for a time in a web of weird arguments, impossible questions and dubious answers.

Seen through this state of my mind, wasn't it reasonable to argue for turning my head, and confirm with my own eyes the existence of the two hoodlums, who at the very second I dreaded, as I prepared for their criminal assault, possibly to be cowardly stabbed in the back?

Then again, something kept my curiosity in check, preventing from turning my head. Just the opposite; I picked up my pace sanely enough in the hope of increasing the distance between us, but making sure not to run, and thus rouse my adversaries' obvious aggressiveness. I hoped against hope to postpone the fatal blow, at least until arriving at the tram station, where I expected the protection of other people.

But as Murphy's Law dictated, lady Luck didn't side with me that night. I heard Kolya's voice as he continued to express his vexation with respect to his friend's indifference.

'Say, Justinian, I can understand you don't want to talk, but if you don't, then what is the use of my__?'

'Kolya, stop it right now, before letting out something you'll regret later, okay? I repeat I'm not in the mood. Please be understanding. Right this minute I need a dram of silence. Can I expect this much from a friend?'

'Yeah, yeah, you may.'

The reluctant reply sounded more like a protesting growl than a freely accepted compliance.

Justinian's attitude obviously miffed Kolya. He went on chewing an endless number of minor curses between his teeth against life, fate, the entire unjust world, but mostly against his good friend's insufferable rejection.

So colorful was he in spewing little blasphemies, so metaphorically poetical and heartfelt in his expressions that I, until then terrified to the core of my being, began to pay attention, even smile slightly amused by the man's obvious *literary* talent.

In spite of these imaginative verbal attempts at long last the poor man had to accept defeat, and return to silence.

During this quiet interlude Kolya's foot dragging on the asphalt became noisier and more obvious than ever. I no longer had any doubts the man was indeed lame. And yet, I didn't dare turn my head to definitely convince myself.

The silent intermission did not last long, and once it ended, my incipient amusement evaporated as quickly as it arose, a deeper, solider and a more acute sense of fear replaced it. In the same instant I could feel again the foul breath of the criminals on the nape of my neck.

The helplessness of the situation finally dawned on me full force, together with my stupid propensity of paying attention to insignificant details, in spite of my predicament's perilous evolution.

It is exactly the type of distraction a threatened human being must fear, when the slightest relaxing of his focus could lead to disaster, and thus preclude deliverance from danger by missing perhaps the only door leading to freedom.

This rule of total dedication to a perilous cause applies equally to all involved, to the criminal and to the innocent, as the first would avoid punishment, while the latter the effect of the crime, in the end preventing both lives from annihilation. Objectively speaking, what is the difference between two dead people, one murdered, and the other condemned to death? Didn't evil and good, guilty and innocent, succumb paradoxically to similar fates? Aren't criminal and the victim indissolubly united at the extremes of one and the same act?

I can't even begin to guess why my mind pondered on such useless philosophical questions during the short silent interval in the sinister dialogue between the brigands, when I had to be more concerned about my immediate safety. I remember though, that in spite of my idiotic musings, I quickened my pace significantly. All was in vain. The bandits succeeded in keeping the distance constant, a fact I considered a sure sign of their evil intentions. Soon I could hear them resuming their interrupted dialogue, without any reference to my person, as if I was invisible.

Kolya spoke first.

'Listen Justinian, why do you punish me? What did I do to deserve such a cold shoulder, and what's this thing about not talking? It makes no sense whatsoever. Now, please explain, how can a man enjoy committing a crime if he's denied to brag loudly about it to a friend? You don't want me to open my mouth in public, do you?'

'O hell no' barked back Justinian curtly, 'no way I want that.'

'Then?'

'My dear chum, please don't feel cross. I am slightly indisposed. Your stance I understand well enough and, indeed, you do have the right to complain. My attitude is neither polite nor rational. But for the devil's sake and in the name of our sacred friendship pact I beg you to be forgiving tonight.'

'Okay, okay, I know we are buddies. That's true. I will no longer reproach you anything. I'm sorry if I ever did.'

At this point the discussion languished. Another uneasy silence fell between the two buddies, heavier, tenser and filled with a palpable sense of foreboding. Every now and then I could hear Kolya sulking, almost on the verge of tears. Obviously, his friend's feigned indifference caused him profound suffering.

Even I began feeling a little pity for the guy. Fortunately I checked myself in time, realizing fast that my life was at stake, not theirs. What did I care for the laments of a wretched loony criminal or fool, who bizarrely lost his way with his friend in this luxurious Vienna neighborhood?"

Thus I resolved to walk defiantly straight ahead, appear sure of myself, and willfully ignore the two, although I did not quit worrying, quite aware of my precarious situation. Secretly I hoped to be paid back with the same coin, to be left alone, at least until I'd reach a modicum of safety in streetcar number 41, although in the station I saw no people or vehicles. Moreover, the station was too far away for sprinting to it.

So there we were all of us walking rapidly together in the pre-set triangular formation; I up front and quite concerned about my fate, Justinian and Kolya right behind, the first in bad mood, the other saddened on the account of his chum's indifference.

Then, when almost on the verge of abandoning myself to a cruel fate, life served me a lesson, proving that not all motion leads to evolution, and not all change of position ends as true progress.

As it happened Kolya still hurt in his tender heart, had to reaffirm his dissatisfaction. Yes, although he professed to understand his friend's desire for privacy, in truth the wretched character itched for more elaborate explanations. He had to resume his probing.

'Listen Justinian, did I somehow get on your nerves? Be frank.'

'No Kolya, you did nothing wrong.'

'Could it be that earlier in the park I showed a bit too eager in murdering the guy? You know well I can be a little selfish every now and then, blind to your feelings because of my ill temper. I am sorry. Tell me, did I rush the killing before you could do it? Is that it? Did I act too fast?'

'No, by all means that's not it. Kolya, stop this silliness. You know me better than that, don't you?'

'Yes, yes, I know and trust you with my life, just want to make sure. You know how much our friendship means to me__ so don't mind my doubting you. Okay? I've just wonder whether my greedy haste prevented you from wasting the infant yourself.'

'Kolya, leave me alone. I beg you to quit this nauseous lamenting, and stop being so puerile.'

'Fine, fine, I stop. But I must ask you once more. Aren't you angry with me at all?'

'No, no, no, and no, I have nothing against you. I AM NOT ANGRY.'

To judge by Justinian's raised voice Kolya's insistence seemed to really annoy him.

'Then what's wrong?'

'What's wrong what?'

By now they were yelling so near to my ears that my over tensed nerves finally gave way, my resistance shattered.

Unhinged, I lost my composure; I threw overboard my feigned indifference, as well as my well-reckoned caution. The moment called for an intervention. I had to end one way or other the impossible situation that apparently embroiled me as in a spider's web. With my dignity violently brought to the fore I itched to put the bums in their proper place. In my judgement the need to reaffirm my privacy rights became surprisingly acute. Sickened by the hoodlums' disgusting, base and stupid dialogue I had to take a firm position. I could no longer accept with indifference their abusive invasion causing noxious effects to my soul's health. What the hell, I was the proud son of a decent mother and father, not some stolen merchandise.

I stopped abruptly, and turned one hundred and eighty degrees on my heels, almost provoking a collision with the two goons.

Caught in surprise, they froze on the spot, desperately and comically trying to regain their balance. Taking advantage of the confusion I addressed them in the sternest possible manner, my tone obviously indignant.

'Gentlemen, please be so kind and keep a decent distance between us.'

In spite of my suddenly impulsive indignation, I tried at the same time to be firm and polite.

'Do not think for a second that I am interested in the least in your affairs. Stop forcing on me your ridiculous conversation. My only wish is to be on my way peacefully without your abusive intrusions into my private space. I want nothing more than that, okay? Good-bye.'

Then without another word I resumed my walk towards the tram station. I felt vaguely satisfied by my daring outburst, also a bit scarred by the consequences of my tempestuous decision, to verbally tackle the crazy idiots, perhaps criminally inclined.

I glanced back. The effect of my intervention occurred with lightening speed and force.

My customers froze on the spot I surprised them. They shrugged their shoulders and exchanged a few looks as dumbfounded. Profiting from my momentary victory, I quickened my pace, and weighed my situation anew.

As it seemed, what I did confused the pair and interrupted their dialogue. This emboldened me to hasten my escape. If nothing else, I succeeded in placing a greater distance between us. Back on my way, I redoubled my efforts, hoping to get rid of the unpleasant company for good.

Only then what I saw seconds earlier hit me in earnest. No doubt, I had to deal with mental cases, individuals probably escaped from a nearby asylum for the insane.

I happened to cast my eyes on Kolya first. He seemed middle aged, an olive skinned raggedy guy with a course, square face. Under his flat and vertically furrowed forehead, bushy black eyebrows grew together at the root of the fleshy nose, squeezed between smoldering dots of coal, his eyes; two dark holes open to the abyss of hell. Between the nose and the extremely thick bluish-red lips, the ruffian sported a moustache of coarse sparsely planted bristles, arched wide over the mouth. The permanently moist lips drooled abundantly over the squarely chiseled chin, populated by the same type of rarified hairs as of the moustache. Kolya was tall, bonny and slightly stooping. All in all, he exuded the threatening and comical allure of some monstrous figures that may be born only in the depths of darkest nightmares. A well-worn furry hat covered the disproportionately tinny head for the man's thick neck and huge body. Above the large, loose pants of formerly red silk, the guy wore a black collarless shirt the Russians call it *rubashka*. Soft leather boots covered the legs up to the knees. In *toto*, the guy's vestments looked old, raggedy, and dirty to the point of meshing colors in one hardly distinguishable mass.

And what a surprise, in a strange mind-boggling but unexplainable fashion, Kolya's figure reminded vaguely of Charles Bronson, not at all of Peter Ustinov, as his voice suggested.

Justinian didn't appear very handsome either. What struck first was the face, absolutely glabrous. His albino-like complexion made me think of a colorless leaf pressed in a herbarium; the features designed as in a child's drawing; the slanted eyes brow-less, the blade-like thin nose hooked, the line-thin lips viciously curved towards the large flapping ears. All these features together created an expression eternally frozen in a perversely malefic grimace. A bright small-size red fez held on precariously to his egg shaped shining bald skull. But the clothing, also of silk, appeared newer, and not as dirty or raggedy as Kolya's. Justinian reminded of a clown, or rather of a harlequin; yellow, green and red-checkered shirt and trousers, feet shod with upward pointed slippers, tipped with white feathery pompons. A dark, well-harmonized crimson belt parted the blouse from the pants; on the right hip hung a scimitar at the end of a thick, orange colored rope. The man's fingers - adorned ostentatiously by several expensive looking, but probably fake rings and imitation stones -, rested habitually on the blade's golden handle. Had he had a moustache, he could have easily brought to mind a debased Vlad the

Impaller, as the fearsome prince might have looked just freed from the Ottoman Aedicule dungeons.

For a second I thought myself in a dream. I couldn't believe my senses, as if I had to deal with Ivan Turbincă and Nastratin Hodja[2], jumped directly off the pages of Ion Creangă's[3] fairy tale.

Be that as it may, I took heed not to let myself overly lured in wonder, and strove to increase distance between them and me.

Once I achieved this, I thought to have plenty of time for figuring out what I saw, and either forget the damned evildoers, or report them to the authorities, which I suspected were searching for them. As for the heinous crimes Kolya purportedly committed, I imagined to be productions of a disturbed mind. Thinking this way I hoped to reestablish my peace of mind and soul. For acting correctly I needed to be cool and calm.

Unfortunately my strategy proved far from adequate.

My overheated heart kept pounding savagely up in my throat, my entire being alternated between icy shivers and hot flashes, while beads of sweat broke out on my forehead. In spite of my faultless logic, my fear didn't let up. Naturally, instinct proved stronger than reasoning, and emphatically so.

It did not take the hoodlums a long time to realize what happened. My cunning strategy probably irked them, and they took after me with renewed vigor. In less than a few minutes they closed the distance, and to my chagrin, I found myself framed, my arms clutched on each side in their tight grips. Suddenly all possibilities for my escape had been foreclosed.

"Well, this is the end," I thought, desperately trying to maintain calm and courage.

I heard Justinian address his friend Kolya over my head.

'Did you hear, my friend? The guy wants to be left alone. You heard him say it, didn't you Kolya?'

'Yeah, I sure did.'

'You must have also heard how much his disliked our tales, right?'

'Indeed, I did.'

---

2   Romanian and Turkish folk heres
3   19 century Romanian classic

'So then, as the civilized and polite guys we are, shouldn't we respect this gentleman's wish, ask for his pardon, go our own ways, and no longer disturb him for inadvertently crossing his paths? What do you say, Kolya?'

Justinian's spoke in a deprecating manner; the words flowed out of his mouth highly inflected, and fell now sweet, now sharp on my acutely sensitized eardrums.

'Right you are Justinian. Let's set him loose, and see how this smart-Alec will cope without us on the dark, deserted streets. Whose help will he ask for, when, God forbid, he might be attacked?'

'True Kolya, who else would jump to this night bird's defense if not us?'

This question hovered suspended an instant in the air unanswered; only to be drowned next into the ever-increasing density of night, while the desperation in my soul shrank to nothingness at the imminence of my inevitable fate.

The reinforced squeeze on my arms clearly confirmed my dim suspicions. The hoodlums showed no sign to set me loose, as they so gallantly proposed just seconds earlier.

From then on I felt vanquished, absolutely certain about my impending death. My lucid reasoning failed altogether.

Automatically I chose to walk in perfect cadence with my oppressors, and no longer resist in any fashion. Void of any feeling I gave myself up to destiny, awaiting its strike as a poor beast taken to the slaughterhouse.

On the silent, dark, deserted street, the sounds of our monotonous steps echoed louder than ever, even Kolya's tortured muffled feet dragging, together with my own well-syncopated stride. Justinian's I couldn't hear at all, for he walked as if on air cushion.

This marching in the twilight that couldn't have lasted very long, appeared to me an eternity. But then I got slowly used to the situation's gravity, and recovered a bit of courage, especially when I noticed no change in our direction.

We were still approaching my initial destination, the streetcar station. A tinny ray of hope re-kindled in my soul, thoroughly benumbed just minutes earlier. My reasoning came back to life, the mind set to work again, my hope hitched to the proverbial piece of straw. I started to weave renewed plans of escape.

We were about to pass by the Inn called *Zum Turkischen Loch,* housed in a decrepit, one-story building the city planners strangely overlooked in the elegant neighborhood for it might have served the needs of jolly *burgers,* still clamoring for the traditional Austrian way. The green wreath signaling fresh wine was vaguely visible in the yellow spotlight approximately trained on it.

Miraculously, the establishment appeared open, unlike the previous nights, when I wanted to dine in there before returning to my hotel downtown. Hoping against hope I thought this to be a good omen.

Suddenly alive, more than ever in my life, I put on the brakes to a screech, and tore violently off the grip of my captors. Surprising even for me this quick, firm decision forced them to stop too.

I took advantage of the ensuing confusion, and said in one breath.

"Gentleman, I feel terribly hungry, so I must thank you for the help, and bid you farewell. Moreover, here I have to make an important phone call. Good bye."

This said I reached for the large tarnished bronze door handle, in my estimation at least a couple hundred years old. I felt saved.

But my haste proved futile. The solution to my difficulty couldn't be that easy. This time around, the two recovered quickly from their consternation, and solicitously hurried to push their hands on mine, wishing *naturally* to help, in the *friendliest* but firmest possible manner. It was Justinian who took the lead, and spoke to me, affecting a reproachful tone.

'Not so fast mister, you shouldn't bid us goodbye so soon. It be a shame to do so, neither be it polite.' Then towards his buddy, 'Hey Kolya, can we allow our friend continue his trip alone, after we provided for his safety this far on the dark dangerous streets? I bet you agree, we can't do that'

'Right you are brother Justinian. How could we desert a fellow human being just like that, at the spur of a whim? We are not that kind of people. I have a proposal. Let us all go in this dump, drink a glass or two of wine together, have a bite, and perhaps listen to some music. What the hell, aren't we decent enough to offer this much to a new friend?'

'My good buddy, this is exactly where I want you to be; generous, hospitable, and solicitous.' Then Justinian turned his attention to me, and spoke on the same hypocritical tone. 'Look, dear friend, we can't split apart. Not yet. It won't be nice. On the contrary, it would be absolutely rude on our part. We now have to prove our kindness, and invite you to be our guest, all expense on us. Agreed?'

It was my turn at getting perplexed, so it took me a while to reply.

'Oh, come on gentleman, I can't accept such a generous offer, especially when I am the one in debt.'

For some unexplained reason, I took to their hypocritical game and feigned appreciation for the help extended.

'My good friends, please don't force me into abusing your generosity I won't ever be able to repay it. What you did for me is too much as it is. I am all right now, so you should stop worrying. Perhaps you had other plans, I do not want to interfere in any way __ please accept my deeply felt gratitude.'

Justinian took over the negotiations alone.

'Be serious my-man. Your thanks are truly unnecessary. It will be our pleasure to empty a few glasses in your company. No need for excuses. Let's step in. As Kolya said, you are our guest.'

Then as to a command, the hoodlums increased the pressure on my hand, still resting on the door handle.

Slowly, the heavy oak door budged, and opened wide noiselessly. Ahead of us loomed a long dim corridor, leading inside towards a lit area, a typical drinking hall for the Austrian folk.

Squeezed between my tormentors I found myself back on square one, all escape routes barred. Willy-nilly I sighed; although my cowardice deeply disgusted me, I shamefully accepted the invitation the newly found *friends* so forcefully offered.

At the corridor's end we came face to face with an ancient looking man. A long beard and hair of an immaculate white framed his face, bringing to fore a narrow forehead, a bulbous red nose, and two dark dots, the man's beady eyes, sunk deep into bloodshot orbits. In spite of the obvious hump and the attending stoop, the man seemed unusually tall, reminding vaguely of an orthodox monk. Had not a turban of indistinguishable color covered his head the similarity could have been perfect. But as it was, possibly serving in the double role of innkeeper and waiter, he received us with low exaggerated bows of the habitually well-feigned respect due to customers.

'Please gentlemen, please come in, and feel welcome. The tables are waiting for your pleasure, reserved as always.'

This peculiar human specimen, well concealed under his coarse robe and white hair, made me recall the famous cinema actor Ernest Borgnine, especially when I saw the face the man's deep, menially humble bow pushed in close to ours. Even his deeply sweet baritone and gurgling voice made me think of the actor. To judge by the instant familiarity of my *friends*, by their clearly emphasized superior's attitude shown him, and the obvious awareness of their well-established status in the inn, I knew; they were old customers.

All of us sat down on the bench at the table indicated; I placed neatly in the middle, properly squeezed in, as it was, between the *Russian* and the *Turk*. What else could I have done but accept the situation as it was. Anyway, no opportunity presented for my escape yet. I had to conform, hope for the best, and be glad for being still alive.

'My distinguished brothers, I enjoy the privilege of serving you tonight, so what can I offer to drink?" the so-called waiter continued his routine after we took our places.

He employed the same syrupy approach, typical for some faithless prelates, monks, or hypocritical pub owners, all equally animated by personal interest and greed, more than by any true belief or solicitude.

'I suggest, if you allow me, the excellent fresh and green wine of the house, which must be well know to you, ha, ha, ha, he, he, he__' At this point the waiter winked slyly, and then added conspiratorially, 'I am sure you figured out long ago that this is the only wine we have, on sale by the pitcher. We serve nothing else with it, no dinner, no snacks, no nothing, as the Law states.' Then the man slapped his thighs and burst into a coarse laughter, thoroughly enjoying his own skewed sense of humor. "ha, ha, ha__'

'Okay, okay Peter, cut the crap; our time and patience is limited. You know what we need and like, don't you? Bring us the wine, including the food from next door, and then tend to your own affairs. Leave the rest to us. You know the routine.'

As always Justinian was the one to put the waiter in his place, after which he pointed at my person still scolding the poor servant.

'And remember to treat our guest with all the respect you owe us.'

He wagged his finger once more, and slid to another mood and gesture, smoothly, clearly, concisely performed for my benefit.

'Look again and take good notice of this gentleman. Do you see him? Then learn, and learn it well; he's not anybody. He's a very important person. Make sure he's treated properly. Do you understand? Say yes.'

'Yes-sir, I understand perfectly. Here I go and here I come, always at your service, sir.'

Without further ado, the waiter turned to me and performed another servile bow, even lower than he did for my *friends* earlier. Only an instant later, he retreated abruptly as pushed by a spring, while keeping his back bent as long as he could, his eyes fixed into mine, vaguely but viciously smiling until he disappeared to my barely disguised disgust behind a swinging door of the opposite wall.

On my turn, in the ensuing interval, as my *buddies* were getting comfortable in their seats, I calmed down somewhat, and began inspecting the premise with my natural curiosity reawakened.

There was nothing remarkable in it. I sat in a modest and simple establishment, typical for the Viennese hilly surroundings, where the green or dried wreath above the entrance indicated fresh or old wine, served in the exclusive manner the emperor decreed *wisely* centuries ago.

I must emphasize the word *exclusive*, because only wine could be served legally. Serving food had been banned long ago, its procurement left entirely up to the client, who either brought it along from home, or bought it next door in a carryout belonging, so-to-speak, to another owner, *independent* of the winery.

In the modestly dimensioned mess hall an electric bulb - precariously hung from an exposed beam above - illuminated dimly three rows of long, rough pinewood tables and benches, enough space left in between for the waiter or the musician to squeeze through.

Customarily the musician played the violin, but that evening an accordionist took his place, one even older looking than the monkish waiter, and so tinny and forlorn in his worn out, soiled Tyrolean outfit that even death seemed to have overlooked him.

No windows interrupted the four white washed walls, only two doors, the entrance and probably an exit to the garden. The latter, locked for the night, had above it a TV set, perched so high on a bracket to make it almost impossible to watch. The TV set - perhaps the only reminder of modernity in this Godforsaken place - was turned on, but not tuned to any station, so that the screen just flickered slightly, adding a little more light to the room's dimness.

An intense aroma of myrrh permeated the atmosphere, strangely tinged with the sour smell of wine, and vague wafts of sizzling steaks.

We were the only customers. The accordionist napped. Under his head, deeply fallen on the chest, rested the locked instrument on his potbelly. He slept standing erect, leaning against the central post, a lone verticality grown out of the clay floor.

I barely concluded my inspection, when the monkish waiter reappeared, bringing along three pitchers of wine in one hand, and a tray in the other, filled with slices of rustic dark bread and smoked Bavarian ham. What the hell, in less chancy times this could have had the appeal of a real feast! As anyone can imagine that night I wasn't prepared at all for partying.

Meanwhile my evil little *buddies* chatted softly, as if they completely forgot about my existence. They lit up at the waiter's arrival. Then, continuing to ignore me, kept prodding each other with extreme formality and politeness to partake off the wine, the slices of bread and ham.

On his turn, the waiter posted voluntarily at the table's end, showed eagerly prepared to satisfy their slightest whims.

It was for me then, I thought, to take advantage of the situation, and reach for the proverbial last saving piece of straw. I addressed the waiter, as any customer might for expressing some humaneness versus a humble servant. I tried to appear matter-of-factly affable, hoping to avoid attracting my evil company's attention.

'Hey boss, please don't mind my asking, but do you, by any chance, have a telephone I can use in this place?'

Naively enough, I wanted to call the police. Who seriously in trouble wouldn't resort to this strategy?

Naturally I achieved nothing other than stir up my adversaries, who instantly alerted, interrupted their feasting as to a command. They pricked up their heads, showing surprised, offended by the daring insolence of a guest toward the hosts.

At this point, something unexpected occurred. The bandits jumped up in unison, grabbed the waiter by the arms, immobilized him completely, then Kolya quickly unsheathed his dagger with his free hand, and pushed it dangerously into the man's Adam's apple, before the poor victim had the time to utter a single syllable in protest.

'Hey you, treacherous little bastard, you were about to give our friend the telephone, didn't you? Didn't we tell you clearly enough the gentleman is our guest? Eh, eh, eh?'

The waiter, who suddenly appeared more monkish than ever under his turban slipped to a side, could do nothing but rotate his eyes in the sockets. The dagger's sharp tip froze the words in his throat. But, as always, Justinian intervened quickly, and stopped Kolya in his tracks. He sounded cool and reasonable.

'Forget it Kolya, let the man catch his breath. Don't accuse him without first hearing him out. We don't yet know what he wanted to say. My good buddy, give the man some slack. Okay? Let him tell us what he was about to do.'

Following this mild admonishing Justinian acted, too; he caught Kolya's sleeve and forced gently his friend's armed hand off the waiter's throat.

The waiter, barely come to his senses coughed a few times, and evidently still shocked, reached to his throat, where just a heartbeat earlier the dagger touched the skin. Finally he was able to utter haltingly.

'Mister Justinian and Mister Kolya, you both must know by now we don't have a phone on the premise, so__'

'My, my Kolya, you got upset for no reason. There isn't a telephone on the premise.'

Then he turned to me with lightening speed.

'Did you hear my friend? No phone in the establishment. Please do not upset yourself uselessly. Drink the wine, eat the food, and enjoy life. Our time on earth is limited. Don't waist it with trifles.'

Justinian sat down, his friend as well, both absolutely calm, as if nothing happened. Moreover, Justinian leaned over the table, poured some wine in my glass, and then handed me the tray with the bread and ham.

'Here, good friend, enjoy the food and drink, and act properly, as a guest should. By the way, who did you want to call?'

The question hit as a thunder, without forewarning, and smashed right against my face. Instantly, my anxiety returned, pushing all my reawakened hopes back into the shadows of earlier fears. I felt caught in the trap again, and this time for some murky reason I blamed myself for it. I could have acted smarter - I thought - had I been more careful before opening my mouth. But now I could do nothing but be secretly upset, feel utterly defeated, and pity myself, of course, uselessly. Thus I replied somewhat evasively.

'I don't know exactly who I wished to call. Perhaps I wanted to find out whether my hotel locked down for the night, before I could get there. Spending the night here with you might cause me to be tardy __.'

'Uhum, uhum __ yes, yes of course. Hey Kolya, did you hear our guest? He just wanted to make sure he wouldn't spend the night on the street. You see my friend what a decent person we deal with, and how easy it is to blame someone unjustly?'

'Listen Justinian, I still don't trust the guy.'

'Oh, Kolya, don't be so mistrusting. Look at our friend" - the man turned to me -, 'don't you see what a decent looking face this fellow has? Look at him carefully.'

'Okay, okay buddy, if you say so. I admit you are so much better at judging characters than I am. You always know all about everything, don't you?'

'Hey, hey, Kolya, do I notice a little resentment in your tone, or what?'

'Naah. Not at all, my dear, I just honestly accept what you are; smarter than me, okay?'

'Oh! Fine.'

After this short exchange Kolya - prepared mercilessly to commit murder a few seconds earlier - settled back into his moronic attitude, totally calm and collected.

I felt lucky. Through his perversely mild manners Justinian once again proved his unusually powerful influence on Kolya, so much so that a minute later the poor subordinate felt compelled to pour obligingly some wine in my glass.

'Come on good friend; let's raise them for a toast. I need to see you empty a glass for my health, and I drink for yours, come on, he said provokingly. 'Let's forget our suspicions, okay?'

Then Kolya changed course, and addressed the waiter, still humbly posted at the table's end, ready to serve.

'You too old man, come and drink with us.'

'My dearly beloved gentleman, I humbly ask to be forgiven, and my meek presence ignored. I am not allowed to drink while on duty. Anyway I don't have a glass, so I cannot___ '

'Wretched old man, do you have to be always so stubborn? What the hell is wrong with you? Be so kind, pick up one from the other table over there, and have drink to our good health. Do it as long as I still ask nicely. What do you say?'

Convinced at last, the waiter obeyed resignedly, and when Justinian raised his glass, the rest of us followed, and poured down our wine bottoms up.

'To our health!'

The waiter wiped off curtly his mouth on his sleeve and prepared to leave, probably thankful for escaping Kolya's clutches unscathed. But Justinian prevented his leaving again.

'Wait a second old man. Don't go yet. If I remember correctly, our friend asked you something. I didn't hear your reply.'

'Yes, yes sir, as I said, we don't have a telephone in this establishment.'

'Don't tell me this you idiot; tell it to our guest. He asked for it, not me.'

So the waiter conformed, and informed me humbly, slowly and docile about the inexistence of a telephone on the premise. I thanked him quietly, hoping to have concluded our short exchange. In spite of my precarious position, suddenly the old waiter's humility, even if feigned, made me feel pity for him.

I turned soft in other respect as well. A final exhaustion poured into my veins; I could no longer distinguish clearly between my own interest and those of my fellow human travelers; a strange condescending compassion for the entire living world rushed up to my conscience from the depth of my chest. Perhaps it was the wine. Yes, yes, I mused, it must be definitely the wine that went fast to my head, causing my fear to turn into sorrow, my reason to disgust, mostly about my own person, but equally about the entire humanity, God, and life itself.

Ah, at that unique instant I could have died, perfectly at peace.

But I didn't. Instead I heard Kolya speak, seemingly bent forever on pestering the waiter.

'I must think, disgusting old man, you lied when you said there is no telephone here. Admit to your lie.'

'I beg your pardon, sir. I didn't lie at all. Why would we need a telephone in this Godforsaken hellhole? Who would we call?'

'Kolya,' intervened Justinian promptly, 'didn't I ask you to leave the poor man alone? Stop the harassment.'

'Yes Justinian, I will. Of course you're right, but then again, who's your bosom buddy, he or I? Please be a little more understanding. I must find out why did the man name this place Godforsaken, okay? This is not a joking issue, you know.'

'Then so be it. Waiter, you heard him. Go ahead Kolya, and ask. But wait a minute; maybe it is I who should do the questioning. As a good chum I will do this for you. Agreed?'

In lieu of replying Kolya leaned across the table, obviously happy and satisfied. He lovingly pinched his friend's cheeks, and placed two noisy wet smooches directly on Justinian's lips.

'This is more like it, my friend. Go ahead; I am sure you know what to do.'

Justinian wiped his lips and took his time. First he poured more wine into his glass, and only then trained his attention to the wretched waiter, still posted bravely at the table, but probably trembling inside as a reed, in advance of the nasty surprise surely in store for him.

'You saw how much you upset my friend Kolya, when you described this place as Godforsaken. If you're right, you owe us an explanation. Tell us man, why do we feel so happy in such an awful place? I hope you see the paradox in your statement, don't you? So be so kind and clear things up and tell us precisely, why did you call this place a Godforsaken hellhole?'

'Sir, you know very well where and what we are.'

Given the precarious situation, in my eyes the waiter now showed real daring as he turned on its head Justinian's accusation. But the latter, totally unfazed, replied promptly enough to stop my budding admiration.

'I don't know anything. Kolya, do you know something? This rag of a servant seems to say that we know where we are. Kolya, my dearest comrade in arms, where do you think we are? What are we doing in this Godforsaken place?'

"My, my, how the hell do I know? Justinian, as I said, the guy makes fun of us. He takes us for being stupid."

At this point Kolya jumped up stormier than ever, his dagger drawn, ready to strike.

"Justinian let me cut down the bastard. He's a no-good-son-of-a-bitch anyway."

'Not so fast Kolya, not so fast; don't be so quick at shedding blood. First the guy must be debriefed, perhaps even interrogated. You know the proper way for finding out what other evil secrets must hide under this dirty cassock. Only after all information is extracted, might your turn rightfully come. Okay?'

Kolya obeyed instantly, as always. Justinian watched him calmly for a second, then took a big gulp from his glass, smacked loudly his lips in ostentatious satisfaction, and addressed the waiter anew. His tone sounded well measured, grave but betraying his barely checked furry.

'Okay sly old wretch, base scoundrel, and disgusting bastard, stupidly enough you chose to employ the well-worn tactics of diversion. What a big mistake! What do you think we are, idiots? Kolya was right after all.'

All of a sudden Justinian leaned into the waiter and pushed his mug dangerously close to his victim's, but to no effect.

The waiter appeared less scared than I imagined. He stood his ground firmly and politely, his head slightly tilted to a side. An unexpected transformation seemed to take place within his soul. Gradually, from the humble humiliated servant he morphed into the proud owner of the establishment, perfectly aware of his rights, no longer willing to succumb to the endless abuse of an erratic customer.

'Sir, listen to me, and listen well, I do not have to play the dumb. I **am** dumb, okay? Dumb because I may go along with people even stupider than I am.'

Justinian didn't expect the sharp turn. He appeared baffled; the waiter's surprisingly cunning boldness stunned him. His jaws fell open; momentarily he couldn't articulate a single syllable.

Kolya reacted differently. As jolted by a thousand volts, he jumped to his feet yelling on top of his lungs, a conduct fit perfectly to the madman he was.

'Please Justinian let me slash this insolent idiot. It's useless to deal with him nicely for another second. You see how darn evil the bastard is. Pity please my friend, don't stop me, and let me dispatch him expeditiously. Allow me to cut him down right now.'

This time Kolya's outburst suited Justinian to a tee; it saved him from further humiliation, and permitted to reassert some of his prerogatives as the boss. He could now again stop cold his friend's criminal action, even if from a temporarily diminished position.

'Hush Kolya, hush! Don't you see; the guy is no longer afraid of you?'

The effect ensued instantly. Instead of calming, as so often before, Justinian's intervention caused Kolya to lose his composure altogether. He could no longer hold back his rage. Having his dignity hurt one too many times finally he must have felt openly the laughing stock he really was. And what ordinary person can face such truth wisely? Not Kolya. Consequently, he jumped up high in the air, not to attack, but to run around the room, while hitting every object in the way with his dagger, without paying heed to any restraint or semblance of common sense. Rabidly foaming at the mouth, he stumbled haphazardly over tables and benches, and succeeded in poking numerous holes in the walls.

'Can you imagine this cunning monkish bastard not being afraid of us? Just say the word Justinian, and I will switch him off in a jiffy. I'll show the mother f___ who's the boss. Come on my friend; permit me to dispatch the son of a bitch to the netherworld right now. Oh, oh, please, please let me do it, please, please, please.'

But then, noticing that no one cared about Kolya's obvious show of lamentable insanity - not the waiter, unmoved in his position at the table, neither Justinian enjoying his food and wine –, I began myself to regain calm.

The light of truth eventually dawned on me too, and I no longer saw in Kolya the insanely crazy man he pretended to be. My revelation made me look at him in a more detached manner, almost with amusement, especially when I noticed the lackluster effect his outburst had on the others.

Even Kolya became aware of his ridiculous position, when a minute later, he totally regained composure, sat back on his chair, resumed eating heartily, and generously poured down his throat several glasses of wine, as if nothing ever happened.

But my total surprise came when Justinian insisted on returning to the interrogation, while meticulously and pointedly licking his greasy fingers one by one. As anyone in his position, he looked intent on satisfying his natural curiosity to the end. He didn't forget the waiter, as the rest of us - distracted by Kolya - almost did.

'So if I understood you correctly you confessed to being dumb, right?'

'Yes sir, it is precisely what I said. I am dumb, that is a total moron.'

'Hmmm, then let me tell you what I think about your apparently candid admission, that there must be some awful secret behind it. Old man, it's precisely what I believe, therefore be so kind and reveal this secret to us, to the so-called smart people we allegedly are. Can you, stupid Dumbo, do for us this much?'

To the end his tone betrayed clear hints of irony and mocking.

'Yes sir, by all means I will do that.'

This was not to happen. In contrast to the victim's willingness to comply with Justinian's request, I observed with increasing awe an unbelievable transformation in the waiter's allure. The man straightened his back; miraculously even his hump flattened, totally gone was his previous humility as well. Out of the blue the former servant appeared secure in his own skin. First he spoke softly, and then as he went on, turned his voice increasingly assertive, harder, and sharper.

'Gentlemen, the secret is as follows, and you must accept it by definition. Here in this place I am the owner, not you. While it is true that the customer is always right, because he orders and is served like a king, nonetheless the final decision in all matters remains to the end entirely mine. Is that clear? Now sir, since you've learned about my secret, tell me if you wish to order more food or wine. If not, please leave me alone; I have other things to do besides chatting with you on diverse esoteric subjects.'

This said, the waiter bowed slightly, and showed ready to depart.

Justinian, who the argument so-to-speak pinned to the wall, seemed ready to acquiesce quietly. But then he recovered unbelievably fast, and held the waiter back with another question.

'Good old man, I must accept, you spoke with true eloquence. You almost convinced me. Then again, why do you think your place is so unpopular tonight? Where are the usual clientele? Might there be something wrong with your business? Can you explain that too?'

'Sure I can. During early spring, people tired after the always too long winter prefer the outdoors on the green grass and in the fresh balmy air. Strolling in the park might be a healthier choice tonight than drinking in this humble place, don't you think so?'

'O-ho, ho, now you really messed up, old buddy. We just came in from the park, and we saw nobody there strolling or otherwise. It is precisely the reason we dropped in with our guest.' He pointed tellingly at me his index finger.

'I am very happy to hear that."

The waiter showed sure signs of impatience. He intimated not so subtly he was fed up with our company.

'So gentleman, once again, what else can I serve you?'

'All right, my friend, I tried to be nice, but to no avail. You wore my patience thin, so please bring us the detector, right now, would you?'

Next Justinian lazily took a badge out of his trousers' pocket, opened it to flash it before the waiter's eyes.

'Take a look, you know what this badge means, don't you? Okay then, consider the municipal sanitary inspection commenced right this minute.'

The new turn caught the innkeeper totally unprepared. He appeared visibly in trouble again. His face turned white as the wall, and in less than an instant his hump resurfaced too. Suddenly the man played the usual humble servant, his head deeply fallen on his chest. He mumbled barely audibly.

'Yes sir, I will bring the detector right now. Just give me a minute,' and the old waiter retreated hastily without turning, while desperately pulling hairs from his long white beard, and performing mechanically rhythmic funny bows.

In the meantime Kolya burst into a loud laughter, repeatedly and violently hitting the table with his fists, to the disquiet and protest of zinging glasses, plates and the pitcher of wine.

The old saying proved correct again; he who laughs last laughs best.

As for me, caught anew by the strange twist of events, my curiosity got the upper hand, making me temporarily forget the dire situation I was in. The only thing I wanted to know how things were to evolve.

I did not have to wait long. The waiter soon returned, bringing along the requested object; a sort of metal detector, as far as I could tell from my limited experience in the matter.

'Sir, here is the detector you requested, but please believe me I have nothing to hide. I swear. And if I don't tell the truth you may as well kill me.'

The old man reverted to his game of being utterly disgusting as he abjectly tried to save his hide. The same second the thing had been handed over I unwillingly noticed the one hundred Schilling note, stuck neatly to the object's smooth plastic handle, which Justinian peremptorily snatched away, money and all, and said.

'Don't worry old man; we will kill you if needed.' Then he turned to his buddy. 'Kolya come on, move your ass, we have a task to perform.'

The two jumped up as if an invisible hand choreographed them, apparently forgetting about me, left to minding my own business.

At precisely the same instant the idea of a realistic escape took shape for the first time in my mind. At the end of the proverbial tunnel twinkled a tinny glimmer of light, irresistibly tempting, as always in life, at the end of all hope.

I got up from the table with the intention of withdrawing stealthily toward the exit, and evade the damned place as fast as possible, while my buddies were seriously preoccupied with discharging their new duties as health inspectors. Indeed, throughout my hasty retreat I could see my former tormentors scanning the entire wall millimeter by square millimeter with the detector.

Soon my hopes were crushed as fast as they arose.

The door at which I aimed right away, obviously there a minute earlier, vanished unbelievably in thin air without a trace, to my utter disappointment it had been totally erased from reality, an instant later, even from my memory. I stopped glued to the spot as a kitten that forgot what it was about to do. I just stood there for another minute totally disoriented, not remembering a thing.

Then it dawned on me; we were all irredeemable prisoners in the inn, condemned each to playing our assigned roles, and passing our cups in an eternal circle, from victim to accused, judge, prosecutor and witness, all at the very same time.

With no alternative in sight, and after returning quietly defeated to my seat, I realized my ignorance about all there is, including about what I had to do next. Confused, I reflexively emptied my glass of wine, soured in the meantime probably because of the increased temperature in the perfectly enclosed exit-less room.

Then, miraculously voided of any worry, neither sad or cheerful, I turned my attention to my traveling companions as to my brothers, getting step by step more interested in their activities, so serious for them, and so inconsequentially useless for me. I began watching slightly amused as my criminal buddies broke the walls, peeled off it the glued-on cheaply printed pictures - invisible seconds earlier -, and how they rolled them up sheet after sheet the unpeeled papyruses filled by mysterious hieroglyphs, visible then perhaps only to my eyes.

I dare say this because no one seemed to notice the relics, nether Justinian or Kolya, both evidently searching for another sort of evidence, certainly less historic, less important, but in the given circumstances probably infinitely more practical and profitable.

In my deeper self I winked and laughed: You must guess, kind reader, what I mean! Isn't sometimes in self-deprecating humor where a man can find salvation amid the worst circumstances?

On his turn, the monkish-looking waiter and innkeeper looked inscrutable, frozen in place, slightly but comfortably leaning against the support column in the middle of the room. He was passively awaiting the verdict of the unexpected inspectors. The old man seemed truly unconcerned, a fact emphasized once more when he calmly lit a cigarette, drew deeply in a few puffs, to be exhaled simultaneously through his mouth and nostrils as thick streams of bluish smoke that passed first through his yellowish white beard, acting as a filtration mesh. Obviously wanting to reinforce this nonchalance, at times he barked out short orders for the musician, who then woke as pushed by a button, broke hastily into music, more exactly into a tune of an Argentinean tango.

In spite of this entire well-performed spectacle, the innkeeper's aloofness and tranquility could not fool anyone, me included. Something in the man's behavior suggested less self-confidence than he wished to project. He must have trembled in the innards of his soul, afraid of being caught in some bad way, frustrated by his inability to interrupt the show.

How right my guess was!

The waiter's show didn't last long, and I heard Kolya and Justinian explode in an unrestrained, triumphantly loud roar. Both released off their chest the fierce outburst of the hungry animal exhausted in the long prowl, but suddenly excited about the imminent conclusion of the successful hunt, about the promised reward of sinking sharp wet teeth into the victim's throat, into the fallen pray caught in the eternal fight for survival.

'Ahaaaaaaaaaa!'

The roar stopped the music abruptly. Taking advantage of the hoodlum's ensuing ecstasy, the accordionist took the coward's way out, and disappeared, as he'd never been in the room. He made himself strangely scarce I couldn't ever figure out how.

What happened?

The two *inspectors* discovered in the wall a secret metallic cabinet, not very large, but ingeniously hidden under the white paint and wallpaper sheets. Naturally, our *inspectors*, just a minute earlier on the verge of abandoning the search, were now elated by the unexpected discovery. Suddenly galvanized, Kolya and Justinian proceeded right away to crack the rectangular box open, first using their nails, than their fists, in the end even the dagger and the saber, but without any success. Finally Justinian came to his senses, and beckoned the innkeeper to approach.

'Give us the key!'

His tone sounded unequivocal, didn't allow to be contradicted.

'My dear gentlemen, honestly, I don't know what key you are talking about. Anyway, why do you think I must have it?' The old man tried again the way of prevarication. 'Moreover, since I had no knowledge about the box in the wall, why should I have the key for it?'

'My, my, devious old bastard, there we go again, playing the stupid, eh?' Justinian did not have time to go on, because Kolya jumped, landed next to the innkeeper, dagger drawn, its sharp tip pressed against the man's chin.

'Hey, hey, dear gentlemen, please don't do this to me. I swear on my mother's grave, I didn't know about the damned hiding place. Believe Me.' the innkeeper wailed as the unlucky thief caught in the saddle of the stolen horse.

'Hey boss, let me waste the wretch. The son of a bitch is poking fun at us.'

'Soon Kolya, soon' and after succeeding, perhaps for the last time to restrain his buddy, Justinian returned his focus on the innkeeper.

'Now *Dumbo,* let me give you a friendly advice; be reasonable and open the box right this second or else I will bestow on Kolya the ecstatic pleasure of slashing your throat. Believe me, idiot old man, your life means less to him than a chicken's. You see I can't control him forever. Try to understand.'

His tone regained its usual harshness, of the boss who does not suffer being contradicted.

'Dear gentlemen,' continued the cornered innkeeper to argue his case hopelessly caught in his web of lies, 'I wouldn't let such a thing happen. Please stop asking me to open the damned box.' Strangely, he sounded sincere, nearly desperate. 'You see, I am forbidden to open something I know nothing about. My action could bring about unimaginable dangers.'

'Look stubborn man; stop dragging out this issue uselessly. You know very well that you're guilty as hell.'

Up to this point Justinian delivered his admonition in a civil manner, but next he lost control completely, and began yelling on top of his lungs, his bloodshot eyes ready to pop off their sockets.

'Stupid idiot, open the damned door, if you love your life. Do you hear me?'

'Yes, yes, I hear you all right.'

Instantly the innkeeper understood; there was no escape. Without further ado he pushed nonchalantly Kolya's dagger off his chin, took out of his bosom a small shining key, hung around his neck at the end of a long golden chain. Then he introduced the key in the lock, twisted it twice, and opened the box without comments.

Flames burst instantly through the opening, as from a hot furnace. Unbearable heat and light radiated into the room with such ferocity that all of us had to shield our eyes reflexively, and then hastily retreat to the remotest corner.

Yet our defense proved inadequate. Soon we had to pile in front of us anything at hand to form a shield: first pieces of clothing, then tables and chairs, just to stave off somehow the hellish fiery torrent.

At last we acted in unison, united as rats caught in the infernal trap of a common enemy, victims, bullies and spectators, all huddled together in precarious safety behind several overturned wooden tables.

'Gentlemen, I beg for your forgiveness,' we heard the innkeeper whispering probably to all of us. He sounded sincere, humble, and contrite. 'Believe me; I knew nothing about the irregularities occurring in the kitchen. Please forgive me.'

Kolya and Justinian did not reply, apparently satisfied to cast a few nasty glances towards the wretched, broken-looking ancient man. Then, they unnaturally and unbelievably cheered up, altogether new characters detached from the issue at hand only to begin indifferently to crack their knuckles.

Could it be that they saw the futility of words in such a grave situation? Who knows?

For the first time that unforgettable evening I surprised myself by the realization of not nurturing any ill feelings against my former enemies. On the contrary, I felt a little sorry for not having the time to know the exotic hoodlums better, and find out what really made them tick. In fact, I thought regretfully, we haven't even been properly introduced. What a pity!

All the same, during these last minutes of common miserable existence on the planet, our curiosity did not cease. In spite of the insupportable heat our organism's desperate attempts at exuding buckets of sweat through zillions of until then unknown pores, we continued watching the incendiary spectacle thoroughly mesmerized by the extraordinary power of hell, ready to swallow us up any second, righteous and evildoers, all together in one sweeping event.

Then another surprise took our breath away.

Through the gaping hellhole created in the door's opening, human beings started streaming into the room; male and female zombies of different ages and stages of decomposition, all slowly and hesitatingly walking toward us enveloped in flames, their bodies rigid, stares stone cold, aimed straight ahead into nothingness.

Clad in diverse brilliantly colored folkloric costumes, some more dazzling than the next, these Godforsaken people – the only words to describe them - became ever more clearly recognizable for what they were; wretched lost souls, with visages marked deservedly by the ugliest burns, the indelible marks of their sinful pasts. Although walking slowly they came relentlessly, one by one, to invade our own proximity, to the point I could distinguish their distorted features, uniformly sorry and sad, as the heat of their bodies burned our skin, even through the tables, barely shielding and separating us from them.

Then I felt the irrepressible need to run away, to escape from this prison, and avoid the suddenly reproachful gaze of these smoldering corpses, perhaps even more than the acrid, overpowering smell of their rotting flesh. But at the same instant I knew; there was no escape. The trap had been perfectly set, tragically unavoidable.

I could not imagine what went through the minds of my *friends* those very same minutes. I had no longer the time or luxury to worry about them. The only thing I remember is that, when they saw the burning human corpses closing in on them to the proximity of a few feet, their nerves shattered, and overwhelmed under the pressure, they jumped ahead, saber and dagger drawn, both prepared to fight or embrace their fellow enemies in death, or perhaps in everlasting bliss.

Time didn't afford me the luxury of finding out the choice my friends opted for, because at the point of contact a miraculous phenomenon occurred, consuming everything in a single bright fulmination and the ear shattering hissing of an electrical discharge. In the same instant all aspects of the inn's reality came to naught, everything vanished, abruptly ebbed, engulfed in the ensuing enormous explosion of blinding light.

I found myself on the deserted street, precisely before the locked entrance to the *Zum Turkischen Loch*; three words the two candles burning dimly in a niche in the wall of the small Catholic Church across the street made vaguely visible. On the brownish-green surface of the door I saw dancing a shadow: Mine.

I was absolutely alone.

The darkness around thickened, the park wafted off a thin, cool and humid breeze. Instinctively I made the sign of the cross and started running towards the tram station visible in the distance; a tinny point of light alluringly beckoning as the promise of an oasis in the desert.

After jumping in one of the two red cars of tram number 41, instantly and inexplicably cheered up, I took a seat at random in the almost empty vehicle. Only then I glanced around, and the next instant I froze on the spot terrified.

Ion Manta

On the opposite bench sat three people shoulder to shoulder, Justinian, Kolya and the monkish-looking innkeeper; ordinary men dressed as commonly as any Viennese citizen. They showed total indifference to my person, all three somewhat sleepy, gazing aimlessly and absently straight ahead, as any traveler would at that late hour of the night."

*

Radu finished his tale, as reading from an imaginary book. His tone although always the same, sounded at the same time monotonous and melodramatic. At concluding the story, a deep sigh left the man's chest; he emptied his glass, and then went into a silent interval purportedly charged with significance.

Radu told his story repeatedly, word-by-word, to anyone willing to listen. Lately, and perhaps unfortunately, I remained his only listener. Gradually everyone abandoned him. Even I see him infrequently, every now and then on Sundays in the parking lot of the church.

He seldom attends the service, preferring to stay in his old decrepit car, filled to the brim with junk. According to some, the car became his permanent residence. Usually he parks in front of the Romanian Orthodox Church, whence he greets a few old acquaintances with a slight nod of his head.

*

Last year, vacationing in Vienna I recalled Radu's story, and visited the aforesaid neighborhood. He was right; silence always reigns on Potzleinsdoreferstrasse.

PARADOX.

(or The Bridge)

I had to spend a few days in New York on business.

One late evening, alone in my modest hotel room, bored and fed up with the run-of-the-mill TV programs relentlessly broadcast on all channels, I went out wishing to spend some time nursing one or more whisky shots in the anonymity of a bar. For some mysterious reason the decision seemed brilliant, and my mood suddenly improved.

Apparently, Lady Luck helped along, since I came upon the first watering hole at the nearest corner. "What a chance", I thought.

Without the slightest hesitation I stepped in.

It was one of those dark, dubious – pardon me – charmingly battered ancient barroom endearingly called an Irish pub; one to have seen better days, but which that night appeared run down, the air inside vaguely foul, reminding of old cigar smoke, and spilled acrid beer.

I chose to sit at a small round marble-topped table in a dim corner as far as possible from the bar-counter, the barman, as well as from the four-five customers, probably regulars facing the TV-set, visible a little above their heads in a corner.

All drank beer while passionately watching the *game* – that is baseball - they commented loudly in the liveliest possible fashion, demonstrating acutely sophisticated expertise, unlike myself, totally illiterate in the matter.

Precisely for this reason I avoided butting in, although I should have familiarized with the game after living the better part of thirty-five years in the States.

The truth is I did not enjoy watching baseball much at all, neither to discuss it, especially with indigene strangers. Consequently, I quickly forgot the bunch, and soon savored my whisky the single female waiter on duty aside the barman promptly served me.

My mind went wandering freely about unclearly shaped thoughts, when I became aware of a presence arisen as of nowhere. A decently clad bearded man, a little over middle age in appearance stood near my table.

He addressed me surprisingly in Romanian, requesting permission in a most preciously polite manner to join me, and keep me company for the night.

I couldn't resist the temptation.

Here in The New World, far away from the Old Country, any Romanian native living mostly amid strangers, at the sound of his own language, automatically and instantly takes the familiar words as a license to acquaint with the person speaking thusly.

I did likewise, and invited the gentleman without further ado to sit, an invitation he readily and unceremoniously accepted with the same ease I offered it. The glass in his hand unequivocally proved that the individual did not approach to bum for a drink. I noticed right away his perfectly tailored dark colored jacket, worn over an impeccably white starched shirt, as well as the properly color-tuned tie, to figure that the man landed in the United States a long time ago. His careless relaxed demeanor pointed to the same fact.

"Mister Băjenaru, in your bewildered look I see you do not recognize me. Am I right?

He was; I did not know the man.

The guy, I thought momentarily, either employed one of the typical opening lines common to conmen - these certainly exist among Romanians as well as in the midst of other nationals –, or he honestly mistook me for someone else. Consequently, I began scrutinizing him more closely, to take a better look, and see whether I could recall anything familiar about his face. Nothing. Nada. Not a single flicker of memory flashed on my mental screen. The man appeared to me a perfect stranger.

"Indeed sir, I remember absolutely nothing about you. I don't think to ever have had the pleasure of your acquaintance."

"It's just what I thought, when I saw your puzzled looks. Mr. Băjenaru, you will surely get rich.[4]" The man had a deep pleasant baritone voice; spoke softly, without a trace of reproach, or being offended, perhaps just a tad disappointed.

As I listened to this voice tinged by some indefinable familiarity, I remained in the dark, in spite of the zillion associative memories sprung up instantly in my mind; long forgotten disparate foggy images, diverse scenes witnessed in Timisoara, more exactly in *Cetate*[5], where I once lived at my grandmothers' place on *Ceahlau*, *Dimitrov* or *Eugen de Savoya* street - or whatever the name happened to be during the precarious Communist years -, years of my childhood and adolescence. I came really close to catching in my new company's pale face some vague resemblance, although insufficient for pinpointing anything concrete.

Then, seeing the obvious vexation that expressed the useless effort of my mental search, the man lost patience, and blurted:

"Mr. Alois Băjenaru, I am Robert, Mircea's brother, your old friend in Timisoara. How come you don't remember me?

"Regretfully I do not. Please let me introduce myself, since you partially did." I stood up, extended my arm over the table, and declined my full name:

"Ion M., not Alois Băjenaru; I am really sorry to disappoint you."

"Oh, oh, then accept my apologies, for mistaking you for someone else. The resemblance is truly fantastic. I hope you can forgive an honest error. My complete name is Robert Frățila."

Suddenly the man's surefootedness and familiarity, previously so evident, rapidly melted before my own eyes into the correct, but more distant politeness of the stranger an inadvertent error forced to beat in retreat, back to the safety of ritualized usage.

"I beg you to overlook my approach's intrusive manner."

"On the contrary, I am glad to have made your acquaintance, and have no reason whatsoever to feel offended."

I accepted the man's outstretched hand, and added.

---

4   According to a Romanian saying when one fails to recognize an old acquaintance, that person is to be getting rich.
5   The central town district, the former fort's area.

"Sometimes complete strangers can show remarkable resemblances, your confusion may happen to anyone." In order to reassure him once more, I repeated my invitation. "Please, have a seat. I'll be happy to share a drink in your company."

"My, my, this is not really necessary. Forgive my imposing on you, but I could've bet my life on your being Mr. Băjenaru, my brother's good friend. Believe me, the resemblance is uncanny indeed."

"So be it. What else can I say? People sometimes resemble some other. I am sorry not to be the one you mistook me for. By the way, where are you from, if I may ask?"

"From Timişoara. I came to the States some ten years ago, at the invitation of my cousin on mother side. He's been living in America since the seventies. His name is Peter Mazilu. You might have heard of him."

"Sorry again, I live in Washington, and know few people in New York."

"Yet you must be familiar with the name. Long ago the family owned a famous pastry shop in Bucharest. Peter is their son. Probably you have heard of the pastry shop."

"That's true. I even sat in their shop, where as a student I enjoyed often the famous Mazilu ice cream. But I didn't have the pleasure to get acquainted with the owners personally. Where exactly lives your cousin presently?"

"In Chicago."

"I've never been in that city. Now I am even more certain I don't know your cousin, nor his friend, or you for that matter."

But in spite of this awkward introduction, the conversation imperceptibly evolved from the banal beginnings to the phase of creating some communications bridges, assumed to exist naturally in the background of our common origin.

Such details wouldn't mean a lot back in Romania, on the other shore of the Atlantic, where approaching a stranger surely happens in less convoluted, but ordinarily more restricted manner.

"Be that as it may, welcome to my table. I feel somewhat lonely myself, so I wouldn't mind at all a drinking buddy. I am happy to accept your company."

Then, wishing to underline my invitation with a gesture, I raised my glass, prodding him to do the same.

"To your health!"

"To your health and to ours!"

We emptied our glasses in one gulp, as manly as possible, the way Romanians traditionally drink plum brandy, not whisky.

"Mr. M., although you're not who I expected, allow me to buy another round in the memory of the friend I thought to be yours as well. I feel obliged to repay the kindness of letting me join you. Please don't refuse me."

I glanced at my watch; the night was still young; I acquiesced.

"Mr. Frățila I will not refuse, but on condition the next round of drinks should be on me. You know, we the Banat folk, don't like to be indebted, and__"

"Ah, ah, the indomitable man of Banat!"

"Exactly."

"So where did you see the light of day, in what community?"

"As I told you, in Timișoara."

"After all then, I was right in sensing to have something in common. This is one more reason to honor the night. Agreed?

He raised his arm, to signal the waitress, barely visible in the bar's darkest corner, where she was secretly smoking, obviously bored by the game on TV, as well as by the noisy clientele. She noticed the signal, and came promptly.

"May I help you?"

"Please bring us another round of sour mash, and don't forget the soda, okay?" and my companion pointed in quick alternation to himself and to me. "You know, for both of us."

"Jack Daniel's as before?"

"Yes, yes, that's right", but then he turned to me. "Ah, I forgot to ask, what do you drink?"

"The same as you do, good old Jack Daniel's. It's my preferred brand, too."

Another coincidence just occurred, another detail to bring us even closer together. The night promised to be interesting. The waitress arrived soon with the drinks. My companion took out his wallet, paid promptly, tip and all, and then raised his glass.

"Mr. M. although I mistook you for someone you're not, I dare toast for your health as among friends."

I did the same.

"And now, since we are drinking together, maybe it is high time for putting formalities aside. Please address me on my first name. I am not that much older than you. What do you say? My friends call me Ion."

"I am happy to oblige, Mr. M., excuse me, Ion. Prost!"

He was from Timişoara all right. The Latin-Germanic way of toasting with "prost" is not used anywhere else in Romania.

"Prost, and to your good luck, Robert!"

"Robby, dear Ion, Robby."

At this point we have crossed the narrow bridge of mutual acceptance, built subconsciously over the river of familiarity, existing naturally between people of the same origin. Next minute we were already steaming ahead on the wider tracks of a budding friendship.

We clinked glasses again, then sipped with obvious delight from the golden amber colored liquid, sips meticulously, ritualistically and delectably chased with small gulps of soda water. Then I saw my newly found friend place his glass carefully in the middle of the napkin imprinted with the bar's logo, after which he sighed.

"Gosh, so many things remind me often of my brother, who__ Well, I must admit, it is hard for me to be without him. When I noticed you earlier, I was sure we talk about him."

All of a sudden the man stopped, as if fallen into his own self, somewhere deep in recollections.

The ensuing interval gave the opportunity to observe my newfound drinking buddy better. I noticed his intelligent expression reflected in his dark dreamy eyes that appeared to penetrate the infinite depth of the soda glass, his entire being lost in a world as yet inaccessible for me.

As I watched I realized having the good luck of enjoying the company of a distinguished character with refined features, belonging to a noble human being. Unknowingly, inexplicably, I grew gradually attracted to the person sitting across the table.

When recapitulating the events of that evening today, I still wonder how I reached this point, the morose and reserved individual I am, why did I allow the man confess, tell his story that he commenced not before another deep sigh as follows.

"In truth I don't really know why to subject you to my grief. Still, dear Ion, allow me to talk about my brother Mircea, and his friend Alois, the latter your apparent twin brother. I am convinced, for no precise reason, that you'll like my tale, if nothing but for the love of art itself."

This unusual introduction succeeded indeed to spark my curiosity. I encouraged the man to go on.

"No need for apologies, my friend Robby; let me hear your story. The night is young; no one is expecting me at the hotel. You too seem to have all the time in the world. Go on then, I promise to be all ears."

I raised my glass once more; he did likewise, and began speaking on the same mellow, velvety, slightly baritone voice, slowly and mesmerizing.

"And now, after I found out what's your place of origin, let's say this tale happened in Timisoara."

Although he barely spoke, I interrupted a little intrigued.

"Let me see, had I not been from Timişoara, the tale should have occurred some place else, in another city?"

"That's about right, Ion."

He fixed his gaze right into mine, eyes opened large and questioning, when, for a fleeting instant, I noticed his fine features frozen in a subtly ironic but slightly condescending smile.

"And what had I been from Bucharest?"

"My tale and our conversation couldn't be the same. It might even not occur."

He lapsed into an exalted sort of silence, but continued subjecting me to the same penetrating ironic gaze, complemented perhaps by a vague note of disappointment – "does this guy really comprehend what I am about to recount?"

He was right, I didn't understand a thing, but why let him know it, I thought.

"If that's so, what if I were a New Yorker?"

"Then we would talk about the weather, or for instance, about baseball, as do the people over there." He pointed to the group at the bar. "Then again, we might discuss politics, but in no way about my brother."

"In other words" – came my vexing retort –, "your tale could take place only in Timişoara?

"I did not say that."

"Then?"

"It could've taken place, for instance in Novy Sad, Subotitza, or even in Szeged[6].

"And nowhere else?"

"Dear Ion, this is not the issue. Naturally, anything may occur anywhere at anytime, In New York, Bucharest, Vienna, Paris or Rome. But the question then is: would it be worth recounting it?"

"And why not?"

"Because – and I became convinced of this long ago – in any super sized cosmopolitan world metropolis or, on the other side of the coin, in any godforsaken provincial town, my story would become meaningless, totally inconsequential. In the first case, my story might get lost in the enormous amount of news just as a trivial fact, as for the second case; it might die without ever crossing the impenetrable threshold of cultural inertia, typical for smaller, unimportant communities. The same goes for nations; the smaller they are the less significant their stories appear in the news. In the larger community my story will be corroded in the harsh acid of alienation, in the remote provincial town, it will be smothered by the rigidly established local mores and customs."

"Now wait a second, your arguments seem too good to be valid."

All of a sudden, I had to find a logical weakness almost compulsively, just to contradict my newfound friend one way or another. So I let my tongue get before my better judgment before weighing things more carefully.

"Then what you suggest is that your tale could very well be tailored to Cluj or Oradea?"

---

6   Cities in Yugoslavia respectively in Sounthern Hungary, in the same geographic square of the larger Banat province.

"Oh Ion, please don't mind my saying it, but in that case we must hit other snags."

"What are you talking about, what snags? All these cities are about the same size and age, both cultural and industrial centers, obviously the same type of people in them. Don't you think so?"

"Look, you just hit the nail on the head. Your two towns are related in many respects, unless we consider them from the point of view of their ethnic mix. Both contain a Romanian and Hungarian component, populations used to an age-old tradition of animosity, at times even outright internal hostility that would provide for my story an altogether improper background. This is so unlike the interethnic familiarity and worldly detachment typical for Timisoara."

"Okay, what about Iaşi?" insisted I stubbornly unconvinced.

"Surely Iaşi must be a fine town, but I never been there. I learned about it only in literature. Although from what I know I dare say Iaşi to be a city with a homogenous population, similarly to other purely Romanian towns that are somewhat wanting in a kind of worldliness, in my opinion, extant only in cities with more than two ethnic elements."

At this point my strange companion began revving up his story-telling engine in earnest.

"That's why I believe that exclusively Timişoara - or Novy Sad, Szeged and Subotitza -, could serve as the ideal background for my tale. Why these cities, you might ask, and not others? Well, because all have something essential in common.

Initially established as Roman settlements, subsequently occupied by Tartars, Turks, Hungarians, Austrians, and Slavs, most are presently inhabited by a majority of Orthodox Romanians and Serbs, a minority of Catholic or Protestant Germans and Hungarians, along with smaller ethnic groups that succeeded together in lending these cities their specific character. The modernity of these cities, uniquely and strangely combined with elements of provincialism, produced some well-tempered and easily interacting social environments, equally related to Western as well as to Eastern mentalities, a feat almost never achieved elsewhere, where chauvinistic national politics won't allow it.

Ion Manta

Few cities fit the model better. This fact I find not particularly worthy for reasons other than the sweetness of life nurtured in them socially, and the sworn allegiance to it by the so-called petty middle class, often derided from culturally "elevated", allegedly more refined vantage points. Moreover, since Timişoara, Novy Sad, Subotitza and Szeged are all settled along rivers – respectively on the Bega, Danube, Tisza or Mures, within the corners of a ten thousand-square-kilometer rectangle that enclose the Banat flatland -, these cities show uncanny architectural similarities in their public buildings, churches, bridges, and all else, rendering my story feasible in any of them. But, as I boasted earlier, as a native of Timişoara, my local pride comes before all other considerations, and for this my friend, I must raise my glass. Hey, good luck to you, my fellow-Timisoara-native-globetrotter!"

The man fell silent, deeply lost in his thoughts. I didn't feel to prodding further, so I reciprocated.

"Good health to you too, Robby."

Soon enough my new drinking pal resumed his tale, which I politely resolved not to interrupt with other of-my-not-too-witty questions.

"Alois Băjenaru and Mircea Frăţila, my brother, became friends as early as in grammar school. They had to register in the school formerly known as *Spiru Harret*, located on Gheorge Lazăr Street, because both resided in "Cetate". We lived on Bogdăneştilor Street, quite near the railroad bridge toward Mehala, and Alois with his parents on Count Mertzy Street, addresses about equidistant from the school."

At this point Robby suspended the story once more.

He lit a cigarette, but not before offering me one as well. The match's flame burst into a mini explosion, and illuminated for an instant my friend's face that struck me as strangely transfigured in emotion. We sipped a little whisky, and my companion returned to his story, as a man resolute to bring it to its well-deserved conclusion.

Soon thereafter, perhaps under the benumbing influence of alcohol and the sweetly harsh taste of the Winston cigarette, mesmerized by my friend's intense monotony of voice, or bewitched by the spell of carefully chosen words streaming off his mouth, the surrounding world, the bar, the men watching baseball, the barman, the waitress, even the dinky room, all melted away into a foggy void.

Next I found myself at home in "Cetate", participating in the story as a character in a motion picture.

"The first days after the classes formed, Mircea and Alois had been assigned to sit next to each other. Although the fact made them truly classmates, the onset of their friendship had to wait for a while longer.

This delay could not be blamed on my older brother Mircea - at the time a slightly plump, bespectacled boy, unusually tall for his age, but an extremely talkative practical jokester -, who did everything possible, silly or sillier, to snare his classmate in his web and make him laugh. On his part, Alois -, a rather smallish, delicate, timid, and mostly taciturn boy with an unusual name -, remained indifferent to all my brother's well intended and precisely aimed, interminable clowning grimaces and senseless banter, unlike the other children screaming and laughing themselves to death, to the chagrin of the teacher unable to control them.

You see, Alois on the father's side was Romanian, but on his mother's German, as his aunt who raised him after his mother's untimely death. So at first he barely spoke the nation's official language, did not understand much of the lessons, and even less of his classmate's humor.

Consequently he had been soon moved to the first row, nearer to the writing board and the teacher. The idea was that removing the boy from the cruel jokes proffered by the Romanian-speaking classmates at his expense on the account of his wrongly perceived stupidity he would achieve faster progress at learning if under closer supervision.

The strategy worked. By the end of school year, Alois overcame indeed his language handicap so much so that he ended up as the second best pupil in the class.

For the budding friendship this happened however too late, because Mircea by then left the school, having to move with us to Orsova[7], where my father had been temporarily reassigned to the project of bringing electric power to villages in Banat.

---

7   Small provincial town by the Danube, at the Yugolsav border..

Chance or, according to some, destiny brought them together for the second time, during the requisite admittance tests to the number one high school for boys known to many locals under the name of Diaconovici Loga. Now, in spite of the many intervening years, the teenagers took compulsively to their seats side by side, as in grammar school.

Recognition occurred instantly. All of a sudden their friendship blossomed in full force, promising not ever to be interrupted. This instant flowering could very well have been the result of the common experience in their past. Be that as it may, the fact is the boys reset fast the vehicles of their lives on familiar tracks. Since recognition occurred in a lightening revelation, it must have also sparked a much greater enthusiasm than if it had been the result of a simple random first encounter.

Less than an hour later, the trust between the two appeared absolute. In retrospect, this could have been predicted even earlier, when during the tests the teenagers unreservedly helped each other, possibly in the hope of becoming classmates later in the fall, at the beginning of the school year in September. So this time around the choice of reconnecting the friendship belonged to them exclusively, no longer to chance.

This detail I find important, because the boys became inseparable.

From this time on they will spend entire days together, mornings in class, afternoons and evenings at play and homework, even during summer vacations, either at the city's public swimming pool.

The rest of the school community became accustomed to this unusual friendship; no one could any longer imagine them as separate entities. Only the school officials, the principal, professors and monitors – more stubborn than the pupils - conspired in vain with the parents on both sides, trying to prevent the further evolution of this friendship -, naturally in the interest of the culprits' education, the two buddies somewhat neglected with the passing of time.

Fortunately, institutionalized studies do not last forever. Eventually, the two youngsters succeeded in passing their baccalaureate exams in spite of all difficulties, not the valedictorians of their parents' hopes, but honorably enough to qualify for testing at institutes of higher learning, as Communists often loved to call Universities.

Those times, when a young man wished to end up not as a poorly paid, unskilled laborer at some primitive factory, or at one of the glorious godforsaken work-sites of the five-year plans, he had to think seriously about acquiring higher education, a way to a better income to be earned later at a comfortable - even if drab - position within the revolutionary Romanian society, "inexorably engaged in building Socialism".

No wonder then that for so many brighter city youngsters the relatively easier office work appeared more enticing than the harsh physical labor, to be performed at work-sites amid obviously disorganized and utterly unsafe, miserable conditions. This preference alone probably explains why yearly some four-to-five applicants often competed for one single position at universities.

Young Mircea and Alois were no different in this respect.

Naturally, they applied at the departments fit to their abilities, although hoping against all hope to study together in Timişoara.

Both tested for the Pedagogical Institute, Alois at the math faculty and Mircea at Romanian literature. Miraculously, they have succeeded, too.

Four years later, following a period of relatively carefree student life - comprising some studying, but also a lot of fun-time spent in the company of similarly young damsels at student clubs, or during summers at the Costinesti resort for students on the Black Sea shore -, they had o travel together to Bucharest, to face the so-called 'assignment commissions', ready to offer them teaching jobs in the country's rural communities, as the contract with the State required.

Ion I am sure you remember the arrangements, whereby you had to repay the expense of your education by working for three years anywhere you had been assigned."

"Of course I do, Robby, go on."

"The graduates at firsts dreamed naively on being assigned to the same school. Since this, realistically speaking, could not coincide with the official wishes, the lives of the two friends henceforward had to follow altogether different paths.

Intuitively prepared for this outcome, Mircea married absolutely out of the blue and with great speed a former University colleague, named Florentina G., a pretty, somewhat bashful young woman, who always spoke in haste, seemed startled even by her own shadow, but who secretly and tenaciously pursued my brother for long years, beginning with their applying for the same department.

The news hit Alois with the force of lightening. Shocked at first he didn't know how to react, but eventually he recovered his self-confidence.

Naïve and young enough to realize fully the power of a woman over her chosen man, he thought himself able to effect a change, to somehow alter the course of events in his favor. He knew that Mircea as the husband of Florentina stood a fairly good chance of gaining assignment in a village near Timisoara. For a single man the same objective did not look similarly easy to reach. Even so he guessed it to be doable. Others did it before him. With the proper intervention everything was possible in Romania the Socialist Republic.

He decided to await the commission's verdict with regard to Mircea, as a family man now first in line.

Although life may bring unpleasant surprises, sometimes it could be equally forthcoming. But when two souls seem fated for a deep friendship, then all complications might strangely work for the same end. That seems to be the meaning of destiny, and that's exactly what happened.

The couple - Mircea and Florentina - was assigned to teach near Arad[8], in a community at a relatively short distance off their beloved hometown Timişoara.

For Alois this looked like a victory. Based on his language skills acquired within the family, he succeeded somehow to be assigned to the German school in a nearby Schwab community, only one train station away from his friend. For all practical reasons they could thus stay together -, more or less.

A year later, when the monotonous reality of the village intellectual turned off our friends earlier enthusiasm for a life balanced between the teaching's tedious duties, wasted weekends in local pubs, or poker games played in the society restricted to the mayor, doctor,

---

8   city in Western Romania

agronomist and always the same colleagues with their wives, they concluded one day to abandon their jobs for something better in the city.

The difficult commuting from village to village, the birth of the first child in Mircea's family further complicated the situation and intensified their desire of moving into a more civilized, urban environment.

Consequently they placed calls here and there to acquaintances of some consequence in the city's affairs. Their efforts were dully rewarded. Following the summer vacation, they did not have to return to their originally assigned workplaces.

They succeeded in occupying together the unlikely and vaguely defined jobs as cultural coordinators, (that is as *methodists* in the local lingo) at the railroaders club in Timişoara.

During the decades of "people's democracy", in larger cities existed such organizations for the benefit of workers, who could attend here weekly science lectures, diverse art and language courses, or participate at organized festivities heavily infested with party propaganda, especially on the occasion of state holydays.

The jobs fit our friends to a T. From this point on they spent time together in the office much longer than the legally prescribed day's eight hours, practically from early in the morning till late at night.

The cultural coordinating activity per se commenced usually a little before noon, in preparation for events to take place afternoons and evenings. On the account of this *demanding* schedule, the two buddies returned home regularly around midnight, occasionally later, but rarely before a repast at restaurants, only God-might-know why, more often at The Officers Club then elsewhere."

"Hey Robby, please, please halt the story right here, and tell me; where did the two friends get the money for this sort of life style? I know exactly what kind of salaries such positions as theirs commanded then."

"Ion, that's really simple. For a few hours during the day they processed photographs for their bosses at half the price the cooperatives charged, naturally in a laboratory and the nessesary materials bought with company funds. The craft itself they picked up attending courses offered at the Club. One hand washed the other, the bosses were happy and the boys were too. You know how things happened back then."

"Oh yes, I remember. Please disregard my question."

"I certainly will, but please don't interrupt, so I may stay faithful to the story. Can you do that Ion?"

"I promise not to repeat my sin."

"Good. By the way, if you must know, my two guys proved practical in other respects as well, and profited in other ways from their jobs; they picked up a couple of foreign languages, made amateur motion pictures, even learned to paint. The latter skill they succeeded in turning into money, as for instance, by drawing the ads for the Club's activities. This way the young men possessed sufficient funds for pursuing their fun-filled life styles, and still bring home intact their salaries, measly as you said they were. Ion, in a relative sense, life treated them well, modeled vaguely along the style of Ilf & Petroff's grand operator "Ostap Bender[9]". I am sure you read the books."

I nodded, and Robby continued.

"Thus it didn't take long for the circle of friends to expand, and for my characters to become quite popular among the town's people, not only intrigued, but amused by the noisy, passionate, always sharply disputed debates carried on in the club, restaurants, or often, even on the streets.

Yet, as much as Mircea and Alois pitched their discussions to extreme levels of polarization, they carefully avoided politics, you know, for obvious reasons. They were wise enough to let the arguments revolve mostly around vaguely philosophical issues.

But what I must emphasize is that when Mircea opted for one intellectual position, Alois chose precisely the opposite, when one depicted a thing white the other made it black, when one believed in the souls' eternity the other didn't see the smallest spark of light surviving death, when one wanted art for art's sake the other pleaded for the power of the message, and so on ad nauseam.

There was something else. As it appeared, they employed another strategy, to limit the discussions to themselves. Whether they decided

---

9 Ostap Bender is the main character in Ilf and Petrov's famous novels, The Golden Calf, and the Twelve Chairs, describing the life of an enterprising „operator" in the Soviet Union of the late twenties.

on this secretly or intuitively I don't know. However it was clear to anyone that the minute a third party dared to butt in the debates, they suddenly joined forces, and never relented until achieving a total, merciless victory over the intruder, whatever his opinions were, reasonable or not.

You can see now why this friendship became famous in the city. No one could imagine them separated.

One day during a habitual evening stroll on the *Corso*[10], a young woman stopped, and said to her boyfriend: 'Look George, these are the guys I talked about earlier, Mircea and Alois'. Then the woman burst into a roaring laughter, while the two didn't even notice, infinitely more involved in their own controversy than to paying attention to the weird reaction of an unknown fellow citizen.

To nobody's surprise Mircea begun neglecting his wife. He got used to seeing her only at nights, mostly in the conjugal bed, which caused the family, slowly but surely, to expand furiously, each year with another little baby boy. The process didn't end before the couple had been blessed with four sons, all comically named Mircea – the First, the Second, the Third and the Fourth. This haphazard, unpremeditated, joke-like suggestion originated with Alois, and Mircea not only accepted it but adopted enthusiastically, unquestioningly in a totally *dada* style, as one should have from a friend.

Poor Florentina, Mircea's wife! She had to condone silently her husband's strange behavior, as the faithful and obedient wife she was, who loved desperately and unconditionally, according to long demoded customs.

Strangely enough, in the end the only person worried about Mircea's marriage was Alois. He must have felt a bit guilty seeing through the fake façade Florentina's pretended unnatural cheerfulness presented publicly. He must have been well aware too about who was partly to blame for her well-dissimulated sadness. He felt the need to search for a correcting solution. Marred by his conscience, he wanted nothing less than to find a wife too, one willing to befriend Florentina as much as he did Mircea. Unusual strategy, isn't it?

---

10   The promenade in some European cities.

But fate hadn't offered any help. Alois enjoyed no success whatsoever with the opposite sex. Women proved smarter than falling into his naively, ridiculously and deceptively spun webs of seduction.

As pangs of conscience come and go, this happened also to Alois, no exception in this sense. Remorse mostly tortured the guy after some heavy drinking bouts, when he felt guilty, and twirled alone in bed at night, saddened about Florentina's fate he allegedly caused. Other times, when in a better mood and not under the influence of wine rushing noxiously through his overheated veins, he tried to justify his behavior rationally, but equally unsuccessfully."

"Well, well, didn't you present Alois' torment as a little too far fetched?" I broke my promise interrupting Robby again. "Nobody can be this stupid."

"Just a second Ion, please wait for the conclusion. Nothing in this world lasts forever; neither did Alois' haphazard fits of remorse. By each passing day, when his pangs of conscience became routine, he gradually but surely forgot Florentina's sorrow, overcome by man's natural indifference.

Eventually the drug of this unusual friendship took over every other concern, barring the two from ever integrating smoothly in the so-called decent proletarian society, increasingly narrower in scope, ever more restricting, tortuous and bland, following the Soviets invasion of Czechoslovakia. And since trouble always comes in pairs, they managed to get hold of an automobile."

"With what money?"

"There you go again. Please Ion, be patient. Prost!"

Fortunately, for Robby the break appeared suddenly appropriate for having another sip of Jack Daniel's. Then the story resumed its course.

"It happened to be the year when the Romanian government launched its domestic automobile production in Colibaşi near Piteşti. Obviously, the first serious buyer was the ever-present state, which in the name of Socialist wisdom decided to renew its decrepit fleet of vehicles. For achieving this goal, the same state had in the meantime to get rid of the old fleet. This was conveniently achieved through selling off the old rundown vehicles to the general public at advantageous terms. This is precisely the offer Mircea and Alois exploited promptly.

They purchased together a beaten up *Renault Dauphin* from the National Theatre in Timişoara, against monthly payments of thirty *lei*[11] that was less than the price of one-kilogram prime quality meat, when officially available in the butcher shops. I assume you recall this sorry state of affairs in Socialist Romania.

But what you certainly can't know is that less than six months later, following much headache, and back-breaking labor for fixing the car, the two friends succeeded in passing it through the technical inspection, and the legal formalities necessary for licensing.

From this point forward they became the Siamese twins truly inseparable. When in the past they were for long hours together within the city limits, in their car they often ventured off the immediate city surroundings, at times farther away, occasionally as far as the Herculaneum Spa, Semenic, Oraviţa or Buziaş[12].

To make my story brief, Mircea and Alois adopted a truly enviable lifestyle, given the usual drabness of building Socialism, perpetually engaged in the fulfillment of the customary five-year plans."

"Hey Ion, prost!" halted Robby his story of his own accord, and raised his glass for another toast.

"Prost!" I replied, abruptly brought back to Queens, into the bar's dark and stale atmosphere, the fringes of Timişoara vanishing fast into the past, suddenly reduced to a tinny luminous spot at the opposite end of the proverbially indomitable present's tunnel.

"Hey waitress, would you please bring us another round?"

Then, for several long seconds, a curtain of eerie silence fell between us, gravely and solemnly pushing the world into our own recollections. But when this heavy silence became overbearing, I felt the need to break the tension, and say something, maybe ask a question, or do just about anything to help my partner resume his tale.

Unfortunately, my nature was as usually not forthcoming. I often behaved lost at such occasions, looking as an idiot, my imagination short-circuited, and my mind void of any creative thinking or

---

11   Leu, the official Romanian currency.
12   Tourist attractions in Banat..

saving spontaneity, as the moron I was, incapable of a natural, quick emotional intercourse. Well this is who I am, and I have to live with it. Luckily, my awkwardness went unnoticed.

My new friend Robby appeared equally lost in his own world of bittersweet memories. His gaze froze at an indefinite point on the tabletop, while his right index finger executed circles on the glass's rim until it begun vibrating.

A uniquely seraphic, weirdly obsessive singsong arose in the room, which sucked the air out of the bar, moving reality into an altogether different dimension. The phenomena could have lasted forever, were we - so-to-speak - not saved by the bell, by the arrival of the waitress with the drinks.

Reality rushed back instantly, I became acutely aware of the scene, as I followed my friend paying the bill, handing over the required tip, and then turning his slightly dimmed, dazed, and almost empty gaze into mine, ready to resume his tale.

"That evening, as so often, I shared the table with Mircea and Alois at the Officers' Club in Timişoara."

All of a sudden the story's broken film lit up on the screen of my imagination as turned on by a switch. The bar rushed away, the present chased off into the past, so dear to the wanderer enjoying to navigate on the see of fantastic words and worlds.

"Earlier in the afternoon it stormed and rained hard. On the sky's ominously dark background flashes of lightening glimmered in the distance, the rumble of thunder no longer audible. The storm retreated in haste; swirling clouds piled high above the horizon. In the purified air one could practically sense the ozone and the static electricity. A huge red-orange sun pierced through an opening, and painted horizontally on the sky a narrow strip of high incandescence, powerful enough to consolidate the darker clouds into a violet band above, as a bit sorry for the violence its own tumultuous energy just caused. Thereafter darkness had grown rapidly, heralding a clear moonlit night and cooler temperatures, a blessing in the aftermath of thirty unbroken days of searing heat, apocalyptically announced nightly on TV and radio stations.

That evening, following our more or less regular strolling tours on the rain-washed Corso, we decided to spend the rest of night in a restaurant. I vividly remember seating down at the designated table. Isn't it interesting how some apparently banal images stick in one's mind?"

I allowed this off-the-cuff rhetorical question pass with no comment. Then the man sighed, dipped gently his lips into the whisky, and continued.

"To take matters in the proper order we all ordered steaks, French fries, pickled cucumbers, and bier. Before our nightly discussions we had to pacify our stomachs, preparing to immerse in deep philosophy. That night we wanted nothing more or less than to elucidate the nature of absolute reality, more precisely, to settle whether reality could be trusted to whatever the senses happened to convey to the mind. You see, we young idiots dared to find an answer to an age-old humongous question. Ha!

Actually we proved a little less conceited than that. Before contributing our own two-penny bits of wisdom, we listed all the classic arguments, beginning with the ancients; Aristotle and Plato, the Eastern mystics, the religious Middle Age thinkers, then with Descartes, Leibnitz, Locke, Hobbes, Hume, Kant, Hegel, Fichte and Berkley, to end up with the moderns; Husserls, Heidegger, Ortega, Russel and many others I no longer care to remember. To cut my story short, after some farfetched cockamamie debate we finally succeeded in formulating the big question: *can the human mind ever figure with certitude an answer in this sense, one verifiable and trustable to everyone as the final truth?*

Naturally Alois and Mircea situated promptly at opposite vantage points. Mircea claimed pounding the table with his fists, the ultimate and obvious strengths of his argument being that as long as our sense reacts it must be responding to something concrete. For instance he asked; is it possible for the acute pain, felt on the arm following a needle's prick, to be of an imaginary nature?

To this Alois retorted, gesticulating widely and asininely mocking his friend, that the example couldn't prove anything beyond the mind's perceptive quality, even if that came as the direct or indirect result of sensations, which science proved never to be definitely trustable. Can't the stimulation of the brain directly induce the same pain? But he did not stop here. He came up with a less conventional example too, formulated as a question about the mind's dreaming state.

'Although the sleeping subject sees, hears, touches, perspires when illusively terrorized in his dream, doesn't the very subject suffer the same when *actually* tormented during the waking state? Now, if we accept as inviolable the law of cause and effect, how can we explain the material reaction of an organism never objectively acted on, in dreams for example? Don't we deal in this case with one of the mind's purely subjective concoctions?'

But the example hadn't convinced Mircea. He wasn't ready to throw in the towel. Not yet. Suddenly he adopted an overly superior, hotly self-assured attitude, and asked:

'Tell me then, what happens to a pair of clocks in the interval between the dreaming state and the awakening of two subjects falling asleep at the time, let's say, from ten at night to six o'clock next morning? Wouldn't each clock indicate the same time, regardless of the obviously different dreams occurring in separate worlds?'

'Hey Mircea, didn't you hear about relativity?'

'That does not apply to this case.'

'And why not?'

By now the discussion, seriously spoiled under the influence of alcohol according to individual temperaments and sensibilities, was slowly and surely sliding down the slope of divagations on the nature of the Cosmic Mind, the entire debate caught in the trappings of the materialist, determinist, or idealist webs, in the vagaries of an age-old philosophical question, probably never to be acceptably answered to everyone's satisfaction.

Who could find the answer to the two-or-three thousand-year-old question, which the whims of fashionable philosophies tilt one way or another? Evidently not Mircea or Alois.

In short, the night promised to be not altogether different, spent as always in interminable discussions about nothing and everything at the same time, in a mold so dear to Romanians, skilled in wasting time better than other more *'developed'* nationals, especially when drinking.

But once the dispute continued after one too many a glass of wine consumed, it visibly veered toward something definitely noisier and less civil. Both Mircea and Alois, by now well inebriated, shot soon beyond the rigorously logic argumentation, and began exchanging small insults, amplified at each turn utill they succeeded in capturing the attention of other people present, generally titillated at the prospect of free shouting matches or fights.

I don't know why and in what way, but from then on an obvious hostility, mutually expressed in ever-meaner terms, tinged the controversy. Never before did I witness such a rage in the behavior of my friends.

Instinctively, I put and end to my boozing. While observing the scene, ever more vexed and perplexed by the sudden degradation of civility, I began worrying. Feeling myself in a bind, I realized that I couldn't intervene without becoming the target of a reunited attack. Such a sacrifice, unfortunately, I was not prepared to make."

At this point Robby suspended his tale for another sip of whiskey. He lifted his glass, and then stopped in midair without touching the glass to his lips. Then he replaced the drink on the table, only to let off his chest another deep sigh, unambiguously more sorrow-filled than ever before. I silently respected the man's privacy of his obviously awakened old emotions, and he soon resumed his story.

"As I said, the dispute – so innocently commenced – crossed long since, surely and inexorably in the forbidden territory of a public scandal. I could no longer see any way out of it. Incredibly, my friends' minds had locked visibly determined on mutual destruction by any means, no matter how base. Evil thoughts and real hate distorted their faces and turned their shouts to snarls. Eventually transformed into a pair of savage bloodthirsty predators, prepared any second to jump and bite violently into the other's flesh, it was Mircea who launched unexpectedly his intellectual provocation.

'If you really consider yourself so smart and firm on your position, let me propose an experiment. Can you accept this much?'

'Sure, what experiment?'

All of a sudden the quarrel came to an end, vanished into thin air as cigarette smoke in the wind. The mutually awoken interest in the opponent's opinion inexplicably replaced their previous hostility.

As for me, from this point forward everything happened as in a dream I couldn't shake off. I overheard Mircea's reply dazed.

'Just listen, and I will explain. I'm sure you're familiar with the Mihai Eminescu Bridge, and its whereabouts.'

'Of course, any decent citizen of Timişoara knows it. What's your point?'

'You'll see soon enough, provided you're willing to hear me out.'

'Go on my friend, I'm all ears.'

'Just a little more patience Alois, first we must agree on something.'

'We do?'

'Yes, we must agree that you and I get totally drunk. Wasted.'

Alois burst into a loud dismissive laughter.

'Don't be too quick with your laughter my friend, and let me ask; is it true for a totally inebriated person to see things doubled?'

'Yeah. So what?'

'Wait and see. As I said, after we will get drunk as skunks, we will take the automobile and drive toward the Mihai Eminescu Bridge – you know, the Mihai Viteazul Boulevard leads straight to it. Now, in the state of absolute drunken intoxication wouldn't we see two bridges instead of just one?'

'Aha, I see now what you aim at. One of the bridges will be real, the other just an illusion. Thus a dilemma will confront us, which one to select. Is that what you suggest?'

'Precisely.'

'And since in hard reality only one material bridge could exist, the other, the virtual won't be there at all. Given the impossibility of crossing a bridge that is not there, your assumption would prove correct and infirm mine, isn't it?'

'That's it. You guessed it all right. After all, there must be a reason we are friends.'

'Okay, I accept the challenge. Fill my glass. The experiment is on.'

'Not so fast guys, I intervened timidly, 'this could end up with an arrest. There's a law against drunk driving, you know.'

'Correct. This is exactly the reason you'll be doing the driving, and we will be giving directions. This way it'll be safe for all of us, you mustn't worry about a thing. As the sober person in the experiment it will be hard for you to err. As you know, the way over the bridge is as straight as it can be. And remember, there's only one bridge. No one can cross the other, the product of Alois' imagination. I hope you are with me in this regard.'

I nodded silently to Mircea's reasoning, stock and barrel, as my older brother probably expected it.

Said and done, my crazy friends set to drinking really, really hard so it didn't take very long for them to reach their goal. Both got thoroughly inebriated, that is deadly drunk. But to my admiring consternation, even in this sorry state both succeeded in preserving a modicum of healthy reasoning, some integrity of their minds.

An hour later we ventured out on the street, the restaurant's clientele followed, eager to see first hand the conclusion of this unusually promising show. Here and there people placed bets. In the Timişoara of those times such events did not occur often.

I took my seat at the wheel without much conviction. Mircea and Alois, before climbing in as well wasted some time showing off before the crowd, obviously enjoying their fleeting minutes of fame.

Then, after a simple twist of the key, a push on the gas pedal and the gray primer-and-putty-spotted red Renault Dauphine's motor roared to life following some initial sputtering.

"Vroom, vroom, vroom" once, twice, thrice - a sound some onlookers dully appreciated -, and the surrounding atmosphere filled with noxious but not entirely unpleasant, unburned hydrocarbon vapors the leaky muffler abundantly exhaled.

Alois concluded first his show for the public's benefit, and then climbed behind me, perfectly aware of the moment and his own importance. Perhaps he wanted to impress the audience with his brave attitude, adopted in spite of his frail, smallish frame, exuding a slightly effeminate charm that the opposite sex generally ignored.

Mircea climbed in next – the tall, handsome and always popular guy in women's eyes. He appeared overly sure of himself, a tad stiff, but still dignified.

To judge by the enthusiastic way the noisy crowd gave its approval, it became instantly clear which guy the crowd preferred, rendering Alois practically invisible.

Following more sputtering and misfiring, the engine I nervously revved up vibrated ominously; its clattering roar turned deafening. Piston rods whipped the motor oil to a froth, pushrods chattered wildly, valves pinged, numerous metallic parts turned to the same infernal rhythm of the symphony of hardened steel, culminating in the act, when the clutch engaged to allow the pent up energy spin tires, burn rubber on the pavement, and jerk the car forward.

Eventually the much-awaited event occurred, we quickly turned the first corner, and vanished from the spot off the circle of spectators, left to inhale the foul smelling bluish-gray smoke, the perishable reminder of our ever being there.

We raced through the Mihai Viteazul Boulevard, and approached fast the bridge selected for the experiment. At this point, instead of slowing down I pushed - as they say - the pedal to the metal. Our vehicle jumped ahead as an arrow released from the highly tensed archer's bow, any possibility of return terminally barred.

'Veer to the right!' – I heard Mircea yell in my ear what Alois contradicted almost instantly.

'No, veer to the left!'

In the attempt to obey both orders, willy-nilly I stayed my course, precisely straight ahead. At the summit of the bridge I must have reached the respectable speed of 140 kilometers, that is 95 miles per our.

Then the unexpected happened.

A sudden explosion rattled the car, a blinding strike of lightening followed, ending in a deafening thunderclap and rumble.

For a nanosecond, I might have lost conscience. But if I ever did, I recovered equally fast, possibly by the next heartbeat.

We practically flew across the bridge unhindered. Our beaten up Renault Dauphin rolled smoothly on the asphalted road leading to the red brick buildings of the Polytechnic Institute.

I took a peek at my rearview mirror, and to my utter horror, I didn't see either Mircea or Alois, as I expected. Behind, on the back bench there was not another soul."

"Prost!" My newfound friend raised his glass as he brought his tale to an abrupt conclusion.

"This is it," he added, and lapsed into a prolonged silence.

Eventually, I felt the need to ask, a little dissatisfied

"Well, well, Robby, I think you owe me an explanation. After all, what actually happened to your brother and his friend?"

"To tell the truth, I don't know. When I got home that night I found my brother Mircea deeply asleep in his bed. He had no recollection whatsoever about what happened.

"Okay, you found Mircea, but what about Alois? I insisted slightly perplexed.

'What about Alois?'

"Don't tell me Alois vanished in thin air." I made a last attempt, obviously shooting for an explanation. "What happened to him?"

Who knows? For a while the rumor went that he might have defected to the West, and then immigrated to the United States. That's precisely why I approached you, when I noticed the resemblance."

The man fixed his gaze straight into my eyes. He had a wide, persistent, sardonic smile smeared on his face.

A little later I probed further.

"And what happened to Mircea?"

"That's the sad part. A few months after that fateful night, Mircea suffered a massive hart attack, and died in the hospital.

*

I felt a gentle touch on my shoulder. The waitress wanted to know whether to bring me another drink. I was alone at the table.

That same night, on my way back to the hotel stridently bathed in the yellow light of sodium bulbs suspended high above the street, for an instant I felt lost, absent from the Universe.

I couldn't recall either my name, or my whereabouts.☐

A STORY OF ROUTINE.
(or Belated Love Affair.)

Rada Drashkovic and Nicolae Ciugudan shared an office in a stylish glass and aluminum low-rise in Rockville, Maryland.

She immigrated to America from Zagreb Croatia in the sixties, together with her parents, he from Timişoara Romania about a decade later, after defecting during the Soviet invasion of Czechoslovakia.

Their room was well air-conditioned but had no windows, a configuration quite common for the space reserved for petty employees working in large elegant office buildings.

As translators - she from Serbo-Croatian and French to English, he from Romanian or Hungarian -, they were happy to have jobs, and work quietly and diligently on their assigned daily tasks, as the often changing demands of this business around The Nation's Capital required. In short, they had no reason whatsoever to complain about their rather small, puny but comfortable room. They even loved the cool office during the torrid and humid months of Washingtonian summers.

"The Institute for Foreign Languages" - a somewhat pompous title –, was a small business owned by an Eastern European German-speaking Jew, who came to America indirectly, via Israel. It is easy then to see why between the boss and his employees the relations gradually grew rather cordial and the atmosphere in the office quite relaxed.

For Rada and Nicolae this meant a lot.

Both viewed their jobs relatively suited to their studies. For the first time since landing in The New World they didn't feel out of place. Following the almost mandatory period of vagaries life imposed on most humanist-educated immigrants as dishwashers, busboys, bellboys, hamburger flippers, salad, cutters - and, if luckier -, as waiters or waitresses, at last they felt good about themselves.

Growing up among proud and conservative people, both preferred working for a living rather than going on the dole, while yearning to leave these jobs behind, as they often said, for the benefit of *the less fortunate, or less educated.*

This attitude the two never deemed snobbish or elitist but just appropriate for securing some positions in society best suited to their qualifications, allegedly for the sake of the well-advertised Capitalist productive efficiency and opportunity. Wouldn't be unfair to reason differently - they asked?

Then again, as products of the Old World, they resented a bit working for tips, even when generously, sometimes whimsically given, according to them, as only masters might offer to servants. As many others coming from across the ocean they secretly thought the habit a little demeaning in a world touting itself to be less stratified than the European.

But as it were, Rada and Nicolae appeared generally content with their emigrant lot in spite of such seldom questioned incongruence, and never seriously doubted the American belief and value system whereby all work is honorable.

By the same token, they didn't fail at being grateful for the compensation received for an adequately decent living that shielded them from the humilities heartless clerks habitually might impose on the jobless in the welfare or unemployment offices. They were often reminded of this luck when, as other passersby, felt compelled to throw alms at the truly unfortunate homeless - a late phenomenon, which according to some, proliferated more than is justified in the richest and fairest society *"the world history had ever recorded"*.

Simply said, the two accepted honestly the American way of life, notwithstanding some reservations, perhaps typical for many immigrants inoculated with the different serum of social norms of the Old World.

Rada, although still a fairly attractive woman, was approaching fast the statistically relevant age of forty, which made her aware ever more acutely of her increasingly reduced chances at marrying to her heart's desire. Astute enough, lately she has grown almost resigned to this cruel fact of life. How come, one may ask?

Because years earlier, out of an ordinary ephemeral, tumultuous but failed love affair she ended up with a little boy, who right after birth became the apple of her eye, a son she happily raised ever since.

As so often, the father vanished promptly following the news, but Rada didn't miss the guy much at all; she obtained what she naturally yearned for, and the proud mother she was kept talking incessantly about her uniquely fantastic child to whoever cared to listen.

Now it was Nicolae's turn.

Listening to her he feigned interest not so much because he truly enjoyed the stories, but rather due to his proverbially difficult age – somewhere between forty-five and fifty – when most females, even minimally attractive, begin looking more alluring for husbands than the wives at home.

And since Nicolae, as so many males, subconsciously frightened before the onrushing old age's first knock at the door of mortality, he perhaps needed a little encouragement from a woman other than the wife, who – perhaps facing her own worrisome issues - routinely neglected to notice her husband's still impressive vigor.

The so-called strong sex, in spite of a much-touted toughness, can become quite week when his physical prowess is placed just a little in doubt. And women, so aptly skilled at catching single men when young, tend to forget this later as wives. Too bad!

So Maria's husband Nicolae - at his perilous age - listened patiently to an endless litany of banalities about the fantastic boy Vlado's adventures performed while crisscrossing The Old Country of Croatia with his mother. These stories involved relatives, friends and places Rada emotionally and proudly evoked, stories our listener cared little for - or similarly to many Romanians -, whether these happened in Croatia or Serbia. He simply liked his colleague Rada as a woman, a fairly pretty one for that.

It is probably a well known fact that during the long afternoon hours in offices all across America, during the bewitching half day following lunch, when time slows dawn tortuously for the employees, when blood drains off brains for the benefit of satiated stomachs, when eyes somnolently freeze at the microscopic letters on computer screens, then a chit-chat with a female companion might come as a true blessing, if for nothing else, but for avoiding the threat of the ever vigilant boss. Such innocent chitchats can become often more pleasant than playing Solitaire, courtesy of Microsoft wise programmers for the same reason; that is to make life in offices a little less drab. But, generally speaking, men and women relish talking to each other more than playing computer games.

Such were the times when Nicolae found out more than he needed to know about Rada, and she learned all too many facts about his intimate life and troubles at home, details to be shared advisedly among friends or lovers, not office mates.

Unfortunately, the sessions occurred ever more frequently, and soon enough a mutual attraction developed between the two colleagues, an attraction that slowly overshadowed the fairly or unfairly neglected, but apparently indifferent wife at home.

Nicolae slowly emptied his whole sack of secrets for Rada.

He confessed all the ever-multiplying quarrels with his wife Maria, annoyingly repeated night after night during the habitual TV watching together, of how stone cold they've grown to each other in bed, and the tricks they resorted to for gaining the greatest distance physically possible between them under the common quilt.

Eventually it became unavoidable for Nicolae not to complain about even more intimate details that threatened their conjugal life, lately gone seriously beyond the mundane misunderstandings, so common to worn out, modern dysfunctional marriages.

These confessions could have ended up all fine and dandy, and quite innocent, but too often when a man reaches the point of sharing with a strange woman such trivial or unabashedly racy details of his life, something other than a collegial relation is bound to grow inadvertently between them.

This is precisely what happened to Rada and Nicolae.

And so, gradually but surely, willy-nilly, this apparently innocent relation blossomed into a true love affair.

The two office mates didn't act with any premeditation whatsoever, but following several luncheons spent conspicuously alone, or in the company of colleagues, celebrating some anniversary of sorts in town, sooner or later the coworkers, always open to gossiping, had to grow aware of it too. Subsequently, when the subjects themselves became aware of their not so well kept secret, the whole thing took instantly an altogether more passionate turn.

From the absolutely innocent and collegial exchange of impressions, Rada and Nicolae crashed straight into the grip of unleashed instincts, suddenly and passionately projected full force upon the screen of their vapid lives.

This thunderous spark of sexual tension, naturally grown between a man and a woman playing with fire, had to be discharged somehow. And this they did furiously and sordidly in a modest motel room, in circumstances overshadowing their love right from the start with a modicum of anxiety, pangs of bad conscience, and the implicit sense of guilt, awoken in both souls at the same time.

Experience shows this kind of love to ending seldom in happiness. Most people uninvolved in illicit love affairs are well aware of this truism, but as it generally happens, for victims the exploding instinct proves almost always stronger than the wisely advised restraint.

Rada and Nicolae knew this too but, as others caught in similar predicaments, they were unable to put a stop to their passion. They allowed the bodies and passions a free run on this illegitimate track, desperately hoping to end up happy and triumphant where so many had failed. Similarly to all incorrigible romantics before them, the poor pair believed against all odds in the victory of love, as in the special gift destiny bestowed upon them. Simply said, the two birds deemed their love unstoppable, and prepared heroically to confront all the obstacles and condemnation a hypocritical, *envious, mean,* and ultimately imperfect society at large hurdled at them from all directions in the name of the well touted morality and respectability.

Still, Rada and Nicolae resolved not to hurt anyone's feelings by acting brashly. Fundamentally, these unfortunate lovers deep down were decent human beings, known to be reluctant even to killing a fly. Consequently the love affair had to be kept secret for as long as possible.

Up to this point, and even later, Nicolae in his mind didn't cease loving his wife, and in spite of the repeated outburst of her manic jealousy - in his view absolutely unjustified -, he never contemplated to actually harm or leave her.

On her part, Rada, afraid of missing her chance at this love materialized of nowhere, worried slightly about the negative reaction of her son, and tacitly accepted the ill-conceived secrecy pact.

Simply put, this pair of belatedly romantic dreamers readily indulged in an awful compromise; he in compensation for the anxiety nestled in his soul at the fulcrum of life, she for allaying the loneliness of the woman left with few good chances at establishing a family.

In the context of such consciously or unconsciously cultivated illusions, this explosive but frustrated love affair conventional wisdom doomed it to failure right from the very start. The emotions of these two forlorn lovers, much too complex to be justly detailed, were deemed to burn out slowly but surely on the altar of their own secrecy agreement, instead of being shielded from the annoying social obligations, from fetters the two lovebirds publicly disdained more than it really called for.

Strangely enough, for an appreciable time – even beyond the few initial months - this tenuous love story appeared nearly blessed, showing some sure signs of success. No wonder then that the two love bird's self-confidence grew day-by-day. The two wretched souls reckoned to have finally hit the nail on the head.

So our lovebirds enjoyed moments of true bliss for quite a while.

Equally consumed in the flames of carnal passion, the pair quickly succumbed to that type of fatal drunkenness, wherefrom there is no return to sobriety; they launched on the slippery and well-honeyed slope of eroticism escaped under control that too often morphs into bitterness and resentment.

But – they might have said - wasn't this sort of passion better than nothing at all?

Unfortunately, after each night spent with Rada, Nicolae had to return in his own conjugal bed regardless how late, forced to come up with increasingly complicated, ingeniously concocted but hardly believable lies, especially for a jealous wife as Maria, permanently wound up for a good scandal.

On her turn, left alone in her just warmed up love nest following Nicolae's hasty, stealthy, never pretty, but always painful exit at midnight or thereabouts, Rada buried her head in the pillow sadly and painfully alone, still abandoned, denied any hope for a better future than she would have in her life before the affair.

One night, when no longer able to repress her feelings, she just casually asked:

"Nicolae, do you really have to go? Stay with me at least once in a while till morning."

"Oh, what a beautiful dream, but I can't."

"And why not? Don't I deserve as much?"

"Dear Rada, Maria is still my wife. You know how troublesome she can be. What if she decides to hurt us? What then?"

"I wish she's dead."

Nicolae swallowed Rada's quip silently, but in his mind made a small note about the instinctive meanness enamored women sometimes can direct against their sister competitors, licit or illicit.

"Why are females so savagely exclusive?" he mused while driving home that night on dark deserted streets.

The next day he forgot Rada's evil remark.

Several weeks or moths later, in spite of its secrecy - obviously transparent even to young Vlado - this bizarre affair settled on the well worn tracks of a routine; for him of the alternate marriage minus the conventional responsibilities; for her on the complacent surrogate wife's, the only two acceptably available alternatives.

In a strange way, at least on the surface, in their own eyes the arrangement appeared suddenly almost meaningful, their problems nearly solved, even when grossly stretched beyond the limits of common sense reality. They readily deluded themselves, believing that the existence of passion may be infinitely better than the lack of it. Poor wretched human beings!

As a matter of course, Saturdays and Sundays the lovers couldn't see each other for obvious reasons. But this didn't mean they couldn't talk on the phone whenever the circumstance allowed, using the cover of some smartly pre-established codes. At the office, once the relationship lost its veils of secrecy, neither was Maria far behind at home, although as the saying goes, the wife is often the last to find out about her husband's misadventures. Nicolae's regular nightly tardiness eventually had to betray him in spite of all his ingeniously imaginative explanations.

Months passed this way, when on a late gloomy November Sunday following Thanksgiving the telephone rang at Nicolae and Maria Ciugudan residence. Maria, nearest to the set, picked up the receiver.

"Yes, this is Ciugudan residence."

"Good evening. May I speak to Mr. Ciugudan, please?"

"May I ask who calls?"

"Rada Drashkovic, his colleague at the office. Is he home?"

"Yes. Hold on a minute, I will get him for you."

She put the receiver down, and then yelled loudly enough to be overheard across an ocean.

"Nick, come to the phone. Your lovey-dovey wants to talk to you, you know, the ugly Serbian bitch Rada."

Nicolae arrived at full speed. He picked up the receiver, covered the microphone with his palm, and castigated his wife.

"Can't you ever abstain from making nasty comments, can you?"

"Common Nick, don't be so sensitive. Can't you appreciate a joke? Just pick up the damned phone. Don't make the poor woman wait."

Then, instead of tending to her own business, she posted herself right on the spot, prepared to overhear the entire conversation as the true hoodoo she suddenly became. She kept watching him intently as he raised the phone to his ear with a well-feigned nonchalance.

"Yes, this is Nicolae. What's up Rada?"

"Nick, I am at the Children's National Medical Center in Washington DC. Vlado had been injured in a serious accident. Forgive me for disturbing you, but I have no one else. I need your help badly, please come. I will wait for you in the emergency room. Okay?"

Nicolae's answer came after a short hesitation.

"Sure, I'll be there in half an hour."

"My colleague's child suffered an accident; the poor mother waits for me at the hospital. I have no way out of this, as much as it displeases me. I promised, so I must go. It's impossible for me to refuse. You know, I share the office with her. You understand this much Maria, don't you?"

"Nick, honestly speaking I do not understand an iota of what you say, but now I, your legally wedded wife, beg you nicely to stay at home, and leave the woman and her troubles alone. Am I clear enough for you?"

The wife spoke calmly but firmly, evidently resolved to impose her will at all cost.

Nicolae, although accustomed to her scenes, for a minute appeared disheartened. Thorn between worrying for Rada and fearing his wife, he tried instinctively to avoid the ensuing quarrel, but as it was could no longer step back from the confrontation. He had to act fast.

"Listen Maria, tonight I will not stay at home just to please you. I must respect my promise, and go to help Rada. I'll leave right this minute."

"Okay Nick, go. Just don't accuse me later I didn't warn you. What you must you do, the decision is yours."

This said, the woman abruptly turned on her heels, and stormed off into the kitchen feigning dignity, ostentatious pride, and a slightly ridiculous cheerfulness, all mixed; her chin up, bearing straight.

He watched her slamming the door, and overheard her repeating:

"The decision is strictly yours, yours only."

Then, following some indistinct curse words, the house grew ominously quiet, as never before during Nicolae's decades-long history with his wife.

Five minutes later as he drove recklessly jerking the car through the slippery, deceptively shining streets, his wife's last words still reverberated in his mind. He tried hard, but unsuccessfully to penetrate their meaning. In the attempt to figure out some sense, he twisted Maria's words on all sides so intently focused mentally that he barely avoided at least three collisions on the way.

He found Rada in the emergency department's waiting room.

Totally shook up and disheveled, she looked ghastly in the strong, cold, white, glaring fluorescent light. Her eyes struck him first; two deep dark holes open between bluish-purple eyelids tumescent from crying. For an instant she appeared to him frighteningly immaterial, a scary Halloween mask.

"Oh Nick, I am so glad you came."

She approached, and he did not resist the natural impulse to embrace her, arms widely open, as a father might receive a bereaved daughter. He let hide her face against his chest. Eventually they sat down next to each other, and she began chaotically, almost incoherently to recount what happened.

He learned how Vlado, the adored son, played soccer earlier on the sidewalk with a bunch of children, and how when he ran to catch the ball kicked on the roadway, an automobile hit the boy pretty badly. Once the police was called, the investigating officer, seeing the child unconscious on the pavement, called urgently for an ambulance. Thus they ended up in the hospital.

The woman concluded her story abruptly; violent hiccups shook her body and she broke into crying.

But as Nicolae instinctively began whispering in her ear words of soothing encouragement while delicately patting her hair, she gradually calmed, only to answer his sweet attention with a firm squeeze of his hand.

Then the doctor came.

"Mrs. Drashkovic, I am happy to report that everything appears to be all right with your son. Little Vlado had been lucky indeed. No vital organs got hurt. In a couple of days or so he will be free to go home, and resume a normal life."

The doctor brought good news, and then noticed Nicolae.

"Ah, excuse me, you must be the husband. It is good you came, too," he concluded and stretched out his right hand to Nicolae, who quickly stepped aside, appearing confused and a bit awkward, as one who ended up there by mistake. For the duration of a heartbeat he wondered whether to let the doctor know he was only a friend, but then took the extended hand, and mumbled barely intelligibly.

"Nicolae Ciugudan, Nice to meet you."

The doctor reciprocated quite affably and added:

"You may both go in now, and see the boy. Just do not stay long. He's still in shock. He should welcome your presence, and feel reassured. Come."

Then the doctor accompanied Rada and Nicoale to Vlado's partition, and quickly vanished from the scene, without any further comment.

Vlado - probably warned beforehand - awaited with his head high up on the pillow, a split transparent tube attached to his nose, another to his arm, while above on a shelf the oscilloscope blipped the rhythm of his heartbeat, still a bit accelerated. At seeing his mother, the boy's dark eyes animated, and a slightly sheepish but welcoming smile lit up his face. The little man probably tried to show off a little, being simultaneously brave, grateful and remorseful.

Rada, the loving mother she was, bent over him, and placed a delicate kiss on the boy's forehead, without saying much of anything. When she got up, took the child's hand into hers, and began gazing sweetly at her son's pretty smile-lit face.

Nicolae stood motionless near her, not knowing what to do, or how to act.

At last Vlado saw him, and their eyes crossed. The boy held his gaze for what seemed a long time, and still in his mother's grip, he placed both hands –his and hers - gently over Nick's, resting on the bed's edge. Then, as one who accomplished a good deed, Vlado shut his eyes, obviously suffused by happiness.

It was precisely the instant when for Nick all events and thoughts mixed in a senseless mental mush of causes and effects. For a very long time he lived struck by a strange amnesia. He barely remembered a thing about his earlier life.

*

Fifteen years later, one bright summer morning, as he opened his eyes his gaze fell on a pair of humongous sneakers Vlado negligently and much too often left smack in the middle of the carpet.

All of a sudden his memory rushed back full force. He remembered vividly his almost daily stumbles over those very shoes, cursing the day he came into the world, until then unbelievably buried in a hazy past.

Alongside in bed he noticed Rada; her disheveled hair spread all over the white pillow, her finely wrinkled complexion clearly visible, her mouth slightly open, eyes shut, tiny blue veins crisscrossed her soapy white hands lying inertly on the red blanket. She snored softly.

Suddenly, Nicolae grew unbelievably sad. For the first time in so many years he remembered Maria, his former wife.

On the following Sunday, more than a decade of absence later, Nicolae appeared at The Romanian Orthodox Church in Falls Church, Virginia, expecting to meet her. There were mostly newcomers; they didn't know the woman he was talking about.

At last an older acquaintance informed him that she left The States about ten years earlier, together with her new husband. The couple returned to the mother country soon after the alleged Romanian revolution in 1989. Maria lived there ever since.

That same Sunday Nicolae vanished from the Romanian community living in or about The Nations Capital. Then he died out even in gossips.□

Other books by Ion Manta (in Romanian):

- "Cu lumina-n ochi" (Against Light) a collection of short stories and a theater play. Editura Marineasa, Timisoara 1998.

- "Blocul turn" (The Highrise) a novel, Editura Marineasa, Timisoara 1999.

- "Intre zi si noapte" (Between Day and Night) Five tales. Editura Marineasa, Timisoara 2000.

- "Sub zodia potrivirilor" (Under the Zodiac of Coincidence.) a novel, Editura Albatros, Bucharest 2005

- "Ceata' (The fog) a short novel, Editura Brumar, Timisoara 2008

- "Viata incrancenata – Roman Cotoman" (A Hard Life – Roman Cotosman) two authors: Livius Ciocarlie and Ion Manta. A biography of an artist, Editura Brumar,Timisoara,2008